THE ⧉⧉⧉⧉⧉⧉⧉⧉⧉ ILIAD

Retold by **NICK McCARTY**

Illustrated by **VICTOR AMBRUS**

SCHOLASTIC INC.
New York Toronto London Auckland Sydney
Mexico City New Delhi Hong Kong Buenos Aires

For Sahosh Thomas and his cousin Pupon—**N.M.**

ISBN 0-439-33794-1

Text copyright © 2000 by Nick McCarty.
Illustrations copyright © 1997 by Victor Ambrus.
Decorative borders copyright © 1997 by Vanessa Card.
All rights reserved.
Published by Scholastic Inc., 555 Broadway,
New York, NY 10012,
by arrangement with Larousse Kingfisher Chambers Inc.
SCHOLASTIC and associated logos are trademarks and/or registered trademarks of Scholastic Inc.

12 11 10 9 8 7 6 5 4 3 2   1 2 3 4 5 6/0

Printed in the U.S.A.   09

First Scholastic printing, September 2001

CONTENTS

PROLOGUE

This is a story of interfering gods, brave warriors, and battles. A story of vengeance, heroic deeds, and the power of a beautiful woman. A story of blood on the earth below the vaulting towers of Troy and in the sand beside the curved, crimson-prowed ships of Greece. It was a time when the gods took sides and meddled in the fate of mortals.

The Greeks have brought war to Troy and besieged the city for nine long years.

Why have they come here? Helen, more beautiful than the moon, has been stolen from her husband, Menelaus, King of Sparta, by Paris, Prince of Troy.

Led by their High King, Agamemnon, a cruel and greedy man, the Greeks fight to win Helen back. The Trojans refuse to let her return.

Each side has its heroes, of course. The Greeks have Achilles, fiery-tempered and a fierce fighter. Prince Hector, the Trojan champion, is a great warrior and more generous than his rival. The causes of their struggle began many years before.

THE STORY BEGINS

Achilles' father, Peleus, was a mortal, and his mother was the sea goddess Thetis. Thetis knew that if she bathed her son in the waters of the River Styx, which mortals cross when they die, he would be safe from earthly harm. She took her baby, held him by his heel over the dark, raging waters, and dipped him into the cold river.

Was he protected? We will see.

At the time of our story, Achilles is a grown man; he runs faster than a gazelle and is as brave a fighter as a mad bear. Achilles of the bright armor leads two thousand and more wolf-wild warriors, riding the wave path in fifty ships. They have come to the Trojan shores out of the southern seas around Greece for vengeance.

So who is to blame for all this?

Paris would say it had nothing to do with him. He would refuse to accept the blame for stealing another man's wife. Paris could not resist the lovely Helen, nor she him. He would claim it was the work of the gods.

"Fate brought Helen to Troy, as Fate brings the Greeks to rot in their huts and in the crimson-prowed boats along our shore. You can't blame me," he would say. "The promise of Aphrodite is the promise of a god. I was bound to do as she foretold."

But Paris was sometimes a petulant, selfish man. Was it his fault? We will see.

THE MEDDLING GODS

Before his birth it was foretold that Paris would be the ruin of Troy. His father, Priam, King of Troy, ordered the herdsman Agelaus to kill the newborn child. But the old man, afraid of the gods' anger if he did what Priam ordered, brought up the child secretly in the mountains. Only he and the gods knew that Paris was the son of Priam.

How did this young man herding long-horned cattle on the soft mountain slopes come to be promised Helen by a goddess? It hardly seems likely. But it is true. The gods had interfered even before Paris was born.

Invitations to the marriage of Thetis, mother of Achilles, to her mortal husband, Peleus, had not included the goddess Eris. Eris was a troublemaker. She was determined that her mischief would echo through time.

During the wedding celebrations Eris threw a golden apple at the feet of the guests. On it were engraved the words "For the Fairest."

Three of the guests, the goddesses Hera, Athena, and Aphrodite, were vain enough to claim the apple. Zeus knew there would be trouble on Olympus if he or one of the other gods were to decide who was fairest. He ordered that the handsome Paris, a mortal, should choose.

Hermes, Zeus's messenger, found Paris herding cattle. The goddesses stood with their faces covered. It was cold this high up the mountain.

"Zeus orders you to choose who is the fairest," said Hermes.

"No," said Paris, shaking his head. "It's not my place to decide. I'd rather not." Paris knew that whatever he said would vex the losers.

Then he smiled and took the golden apple. "I'll divide it into three and give them each a piece."

"Paris, you must decide," Hermes insisted.

Reluctantly, Paris walked up the slope toward the goddesses.

"Please," he begged, "I didn't choose to do this. What can a man do when ordered by Zeus?"

The goddesses turned toward him. Paris shielded his eyes from their blazing loveliness. "One at a time, please. I am blinded by the three of you together."

Hera was first. She came close and whispered, "Give me the prize and I will make you Lord of Asia and the richest man alive."

Paris said nothing. He looked away.

Athena was next. She stood looking him straight in the eye as, high over the dark crags, an eagle soared into the endless blue sky.

"If I win, I will bring you victory in all your battles. I'll make you the wisest and most handsome man in the world."

Paris shrugged. "I don't need to win battles. I'm a herdsman. I don't need bribes to make a fair judgment. Now, is Aphrodite ready?"

Aphrodite stood on the soft, green grass. The mild summer wind whispered around her. She leaned closer to the youth. "Paris, a man as handsome as you shouldn't waste his life on these mountains. You will marry Helen of Sparta, who is almost as beautiful as I am. Helen, daughter of Zeus and lovely as a swan, is yours."

Aphrodite shamelessly moved closer to the trembling young man. "Go to Sparta, Paris, and she will fall head over heels in love with you. I swear it."

Without hesitation, the young man gave the golden apple to Aphrodite.

Hera and Athena would not forget the insult Paris had never meant to offer them.

So it began. . . .

Each year King Priam held games in memory of the son he had condemned to die on the mountains. He would send a request to Agelaus, his chief herdsman, to bring a magnificent bull to be given as a prize at the games. One fateful year, not knowing he was Priam's lost son, Paris decided to follow the bull into the city. Agelaus begged him not to go, but the youth was determined to compete in the games.

He competed in the boxing and won; he ran the foot-race and won, beating the king's sons Hector and Deiphobus. They challenged him to run again. Paris won his third laurel wreath.

Hector and his brother, furious at being beaten by a common herdsman, threatened him with their swords. To save the unarmed Paris, Agelaus confessed he had not obeyed the king's order to kill the baby. So Paris was happily reunited with King Priam, his father, and made peace with his brothers.

Now a Trojan prince, Paris still remembered the promise Aphrodite had made to him on the mountain slopes. One day he asked his father if he could lead a delegation to the Greek city of Sparta, where King Menelaus ruled with Helen, his wife.

The gods smiled and watched their mischief unfold. . . .

Paris found himself the honored guest of Menelaus in Sparta, a white-walled city in a barren part of Greece. He was treated with great hospitality. He repaid it dishonorably.

Helen was everything that Aphrodite had described when Paris awarded her the golden apple. Paris could not resist her.

He gave Helen gifts, whispered honeyed words, drank from the goblet she had drunk from. And she was equally attracted to this handsome young man.

They walked together through the palace, sat in the shaded courtyard, touched hands as if by accident, and gazed at each other. The court was alive with whispers and rumors.

King Menelaus, a decent man, would not believe the gossip. He saw how Paris never left his wife's side, but thought it a young man's folly. He even left them together when he sailed to Crete for his grandfather's funeral, urging Helen to stay to entertain their Trojan guest.

That same night, Helen shamelessly left Sparta with Paris and sailed for Troy.

It was done, and what came followed as night follows day.

A Thousand Ships Sail for Troy

All of Troy fell under the spell of Helen's beauty. Paris vowed she would never be returned to Menelaus. But Hector, a brave and honorable prince, was wary of Helen and her dangerous beauty—as was his wife, Andromache, a wise and noble woman.

Menelaus demanded that his brother, the High King Agamemnon, help him retrieve his wife. Agamemnon agreed, as was his duty.

So the Greeks came.

They came from Cephisus and Sacred Crisa. Ajax brought twelve ships from Salamis and beached them at Aulis, where the Athenian army camped. Men came from Cyprus, the land of doves; others came led by a son of Hercules.

Still the Greek ships came.

Menelaus came from Sparta with sixty ships to fight under his brother Agamemnon. The High King brought the largest force, from Corinth and Mycenae. And still they came.

From Pylos and from Crete came men led by Idomeneus the spearman. From Halkidiki, Mantinea, Anceaus, high-prowed, bright-painted ships swooped across the waves, carrying well-armed Greeks.

Odysseus left the island of Ithaca, a place of pine forests and soft, blue seas. With twelve crimson-prowed ships, he left his faithful wife Penelope, in the hope of battle, loot, and glory.

Warlike Diomedes came to prove his bravery. He brought eighty black-sailed ships from vine-covered Epidaurus.

Nestor, though an old man, came to offer wise counsel, with a crew of warriors eager for the clash of bronze on bronze.

And the mighty hero Achilles came with fifty open ships, each carrying fifty warriors eager to fight.

So they came—swan-prowed, open boats crashing through the deep, green sea and over the sparkling dawn waves. They drove on until nightfall, then lay to on the lifting swell. They rode, like carrion birds swooping the swelling waters together, close by the black cliffs and foaming spray.

The gods, sitting on Olympus, gathered like gulls over a school of silver fish. Zeus, Father of the Gods; Hera, his wife; Athena, the goddess of war; Poseidon, the Earthshaker; Aphrodite, the goddess of love; and Eris, the mischief-maker, looked down on the Greek armies and at their favorite warriors.

The fleet had gathered in a safe haven at Aulis to regroup before they reached Troy. There they saw an omen. They were making sacrifice when suddenly a snake with blood-red markings, fast as a whip, emerged from below an altar, streaking straight for a plane tree.

A brood of fledgling sparrows sat on its top branch. The mother fluttered nearby as the snake ate the nine little birds. Then the snake coiled, struck again, and took the mother bird, eating her too.

The warriors wanted to know what this meant, and Calchas the seer spoke. "Zeus has sent a message. We will fight for Troy's high towers and wide streets for nine years—one year for each of the fledglings. In the tenth year the streets, towers, and walls will be ours." In the bright morning they sailed for Troy, and for battle.

THE SIEGE OF TROY

Nine years have passed. And the Greek raiders are still outside the walls of Troy. Some of the warriors are tired of the siege. Their boats warp, and the sails decay. Yet they will not abandon the siege while Helen stays with Paris behind the Trojan walls. There are those who say that these two have caused a hundred thousand deaths and led men to rot on the beach below the city walls.

Now, foolishly, the High King Agamemnon has angered the god Apollo. It happened this way.

One morning an old man hobbled down to the beach from the direction of Troy. He passed between the boats, carrying a heavy load on his back. He found the Greeks seated around their High King. The old man walked through the ranks of soldiers with the aid of his staff, which showed he was a priest of the god Apollo.

He walked directly and with dignity to Agamemnon and laid down

11

his heavy load at the High King's feet. There was gold plate, armor, swords, bronze mirrors, and a bronze and silver shield. Agamemnon asked his name, and the old man looked him boldly in the face. The High King knew him now. The old man's daughter, Chryseis, had been taken by Agamemnon when the Greeks had raided a village beyond Troy. She was part of the loot the Greeks had taken. It was usual.

The old man spoke quietly. "You took my child for yourself," he said. It was true. And at the same time a lovely young woman named Briseis was given to Achilles as his portion of the loot.

The old man went on. "I have come to ransom my daughter."

No one spoke, for the old man had moved them with his dignity.

"My lords," he said, turning to the soldiers seated behind him. "You hope to take Troy and then to sail home safely. Maybe the gods will grant your wish—but not unless you show reverence to the archer god, Apollo, by accepting this ransom and releasing my daughter. I tell you, for I am his priest and know how powerful his anger can be."

The men, admiring his courage, applauded him. They wanted Agamemnon to free the girl so she could go home with her father. But the High King, furious with his soldiers, rounded angrily on the old man.

"You old fool, get away from our ships. You'll find your priest's staff no shield against my anger. I will not allow Chryseis, your daughter, to go. She is my property. Get away before I set the war dogs on you."

The warriors were embarrassed at Agamemnon's rudeness to the dignified old man. But no one had the right to question the High King.

The old man turned and hobbled away along the seashore. As he went, he prayed to Apollo. "If ever I made a sacrifice that pleased you, if ever the goat or the bull I offered delighted you, then grant me one wish. Let the Greeks pay for my tears with your arrows."

And they did. Apollo was furious at the insult to his priest, and he came down on the Greeks like darkest night. Mules and dogs died first, and then, one after another, men were hit by the god's hissing arrows.

Apollo rained plague upon the camp.

I · AGAMEMNON'S ANGER

The smoke rose thick from the Greek funeral pyres where the bodies and weapons of dead warriors burned. It swirled across the battlefield before the Trojan gates.

Hera, Zeus's wife, could not stop herself interfering on the side of Achilles, her favorite Greek. The goddess told him to call the soldiers together. When they were assembled, Achilles asked Agamemnon to listen to Calchas, the seer, who understood dreams. He would know how to calm the anger of Apollo.

Calchas was reluctant. Knowing the past and future can be a dangerous gift. Telling it can be even more dangerous. Achilles gave Calchas no choice, but promised to protect him if Agamemnon grew angry.

So Calchas told the High King what he did not wish to hear. Agamemnon had insulted Apollo by refusing to return his priest's daughter, Chryseis. If he did not return her, Apollo would plague them until there were not enough Greeks alive to crew their boats. They would be trapped on the shore, prey to time, to plague, to the Trojan army.

Achilles proposed that Agamemnon might be compensated for his loss if he agreed to free Chryseis. But Agamemnon rose in a seething fury and refused his greatest warriors demands.

"You expect me to give her up? I will not be robbed of my loot."

Achilles was not afraid. He sneered at the angry king. "Your greed is a legend already. You have no thought for the men dying of a rotting plague, no care for your soldiers years from home."

The men seated on the sand and high in the dunes all growled their agreement. The funeral pyres crackled and burned as Achilles went on.

"Trojan warriors never came to my land, took a horse of mine, or pillaged our homes, or burned our crops. We came to help *you*—and all you can do is make us pay for your stupidity. We have battled for the loot we have stored in our boats. I always take the lion's share of the fight, and yet you would rob me of my prize. There's no point in staying here to be insulted while I pile up gold and loot for you."

Achilles was in an ice-cold fury, his knuckles white with it.

Apollo's arrows flashed faster through the smoke of the funeral pyres, into the ranks of warriors, sending many more into neverending darkness.

Agamemnon, in a rage, shouted at Achilles without measure.

"I will give up Chryseis to stop Apollo cutting down my faithful warriors with this filthy plague, but you, Achilles, will pay the price."

Agamemnon stood, his long hair tied back, his dark beard flowing. His face twisted with anger as he shouted at the younger man.

"I will send Chryseis back to her father with Odysseus. I will offer gifts to pacify Apollo. Then, Achilles, I will take the beautiful Briseis, who was given to *you* as loot. I'll teach you to defy your king!"

Achilles reached for his short-bladed sword. If he drew it, all around knew whose blood would run along the bronze blade.

Agamemnon stepped back in fear, for Achilles was ready to push past the guards to kill him. But Athena came to soothe the warrior.

"Achilles," she whispered, "Hera sent me to calm you. Take your hand off your sword. Do as we suggest and you will gain by it."

No one saw the goddess. They only saw Achilles point his empty hand at Agamemnon. "You drunkard!" he hissed. "You have the courage of a

sparrow. You stay in the camp while others fight for you. You will take the lady Briseis because you are High King and we must let you have your cowardly way."

Some men feared Achilles had gone too far, but he went on.

"The day is coming, Agamemnon, when you and your men will miss me."

The warriors dared not speak. Agamemnon and his council wanted to silence the angry man. But still Achilles went on.

"They will be powerless as they fall under the swords of Hector of Troy and his men. I see it. You'll regret treating the best man in this company with contempt."

Nestor, the wise old man, tried to persuade Agamemnon not to take Briseis from Achilles. But the High King refused. Chryseis would return to her father, and *he* would have Briseis. Any man who tried to prevent it would die.

Achilles stalked away from the gathering with Patroclus, his closest companion. He walked down through the tangle of hawsers, masts, oars; beneath the proud bows of the ships drawn

16

up on the shore, he swore never again to fight for the High King.

Agamemnon sent two warriors to Achilles' hut to bring back Briseis. They were nervous crossing the foreshore, past the rotting crab shells and dead seabirds, through the drying piles of sea wrack, toward the hut of such a dangerous, unpredictable man. Small sand fleas leapt as their dragging feet disturbed the decaying weed.

When they arrived at the hut, they found Achilles standing gravely in the doorway, and beside him Briseis, in tears.

"Don't be afraid," he told the warriors. "My quarrel is not with you, but with your greedy master. Patroclus will hand the lady to you. Remember that when Agamemnon finds Trojans bringing burning brands to torch the ships, he will not have anyone to turn them away. Tell him Achilles has sworn it."

Patroclus took the weeping girl by the hand and gave her to the two men. They led her away to Agamemnon, and Achilles mourned his loss, for he truly loved the girl.

Thetis, his mother, heard him sighing where she sat beneath the waves. She came out of the glittering sea in a mist and sat beside her son to comfort him.

Achilles told his mother of his fury.

She said sadly, "I am afraid for you. Fate has given you too short a life, Achilles, to waste it on anger. I will go to Olympus to see Zeus and do what I can. You will take no further part in the fighting, as you have sworn, until I come back with an answer."

Meanwhile, Odysseus and his crew knocked away the props that held his ship upright on the sand, and the men hauled the crimson-painted boat into the dark waters of the bay. They took the lovely Chryseis back to her father. Achilles nursed his anger.

Thetis emerged in the morning light, rose into the wide blue sky, and found Zeus resting on Olympus. She told him how Achilles had been robbed by Agamemnon and urged Zeus to help the Trojans.

Zeus grumbled, "Hera, my wife, is already complaining that I help them too much. If she sees you with me she will be even worse."

Thetis knelt and clasped Zeus's knees in submission.

"Zeus, promise me you will help."

"Oh, very well. Yes, yes. Now let me be."

Zeus was impatient for Thetis to leave before jealous Hera saw her. Thetis of the silver feet dived from snowcapped Olympus into the glittering green depths of the sea. Too late. Hera had seen her, and was at her husband the instant Thetis had gone.

"Tell me," she hissed, "what have you been plotting with Thetis behind my back? Tell me!"

Zeus growled a warning, and Hera, the ox-eyed, smiled in the winning way she had when it suited her.

"Zeus, you know I don't mean to be disrespectful. You know I never want to interfere, but I believe you have promised Thetis to let the Greeks be slaughtered beside their ships. I won't have that—"

"Stop!" roared Zeus. "Learn one thing from me, Hera. You will obey me as all the gods obey me, or you'll be flung headlong into darkness. Agamemnon will suffer for his greed until he gives Achilles the respect he is due. That is my decision. Meanwhile, Achilles has sworn to take no part in the fighting. Remember what I have said and be afraid."

And Zeus in his anger towered like a huge thundercloud over the mountains. Lightning flashed and thunder roared around the high land and over the black waves of the sea.

II · A Test

The gods, like us, do not like arrogant men. Zeus was displeased, so that thunderous night he sent a false dream to Agamemnon. Troy would be theirs if they attacked immediately.

The High King awoke, put on his tunic and flowing cloak, slung a silver sword over his shoulder, took his staff of office, and walked among the ships where his army rested. He decided to test their courage. They were called to order by their commanders. Then Agamemnon spoke.

"Mighty Zeus is against us. I believe we should leave before the Trojan hordes press us into the sea."

Hearing their commander-in-chief counsel retreat, many panicked. They cleared the runways, knocked away the props, and began to manhandle the ships into the sea.

Hera and Athena tried to stop this cowardly rush. Athena called Odysseus to help. He ran among the frantic men, shouting, hitting, cajoling. "Are you women? You flutter like doves with a rat in their dovecote. What are you? Cowards?"

As you would expect, they were shamed then. A troublemaking orator, Thersites, goaded the men and insulted Agamemnon, calling him a coward, an old woman, a thief. But Thersites had gone too far. To insult the position of High King was to insult the gods.

Odysseus struck the ranting orator, flung him aside—and the men cheered the rough warrior-king. They were determined to fight, to regain the honor they had so nearly thrown away.

Zeus smiled. The Greeks would be overeager—all but Achilles, who sulked by his ships. Agamemnon would pay for his meanness to Achilles. It was as Zeus had promised Thetis.

Behind them, within the city walls, battle drums sounded.

The Greeks hurried to get their armor and began to dress for war.

III · A Challenge

The dust of the marching army blotted out the sun. The Greeks came with their chariots and bird-swift horses. They came carrying bone-sprung bows, gold-hilted swords, and oxhide shields embossed with flashing bronze. They marched toward Troy, and the earth groaned. The sun burst through, lighting the spear points and plumed helmets of eager warriors and the glistening coats of the horses.

It was as if the plain rippled with fire.

Achilles and his men slept, played games, or watched their horses. They heard the roaring hordes suddenly go quiet as the chieftains faced the mighty wooden gates of Troy.

From the highest towers, Trojan sentries sent news of the approaching army to King Priam. Hector, impetuous and anxious to begin the battle, ordered the clan leaders within the walls to prepare.

The mighty wooden gates were thrown open, and the Trojan army poured toward their chosen position, a hill called the Tomb of the Dancing Myrine. Warriors were as many as the leaves in a forest. The Trojans roared their battle cries, clashed sword on shield like war drums.

The Greeks moved silently forward into the rising dust, unable to see beyond a stone's throw. Swords held low and ready, spears poised, javelins balanced, arrows nocked, bowstrings taut, they awaited their chieftain's command to strike.

Paris stepped out ahead of the Trojan ranks, a leopard skin on his back, a curved bow and a sword slung from his shoulders, and in his hands two bronze-headed spears. He challenged any Greek hero to meet him man to man to fight it out.

Menelaus, whose wife this man had stolen, leapt from his chariot to confront him. Happy as a hungry lion facing a wounded antelope, Menelaus accepted the challenge. But Paris, seeing who faced him, was afraid and slunk back into the Trojan ranks.

Hector, his brother, shouted, "Pretty boy! Seducer of women! Were you born to shame us? You pitiful coward, you'd be better dead. The enemy will think we make leaders because a man is good-looking. They'll mock us because you have no guts. Be a man! If you know how!"

In a fury, Hector pursued Paris until he could back away no farther.

"You're only good for going into another man's house and seducing his wife. You brought shame on your father and a curse on our city. You're afraid to fight the man whose wife you stole. Your long hair won't help you, nor your precious goddess Aphrodite. You're not worth my spit."

Paris saw only the stony faces of those who heard Hector's contempt. Trying to calm his brother, he touched his arm. "Did I ask to be handsome?"

Hector turned away in anger then. Paris followed.

"I am not as warlike as you, as gifted with sword and spear, but if you demand it, I will fight this duel." Paris raised his voice so all could hear. "The man who wins will win Helen and her wealth."

The stony faces began to soften now. . . .

"Then our leaders may make a treaty. We will stay in Troy, and the Greeks can sail home. I will fight for that."

Hector stood between the two armies and asked them to sit while Menelaus and Paris fought. He suggested terms that would lead to the end of the war. No one from the Greek side wanted to answer. Then Menelaus spoke.

"I have suffered most in all of this. I agree that Trojans and Greeks can make peace. The real feud is between Paris and me. One of us must die. Fate decrees it will be him. Bring sacrifices. And bring King Priam to witness the oath. We don't trust his sons to make a binding promise. Bring a ram and a ewe and let the oaths be sworn."

The warriors roared their approval and sat facing each other.

Helen and Andromache, Hector's wife, watched from the towers over the gates of Troy. Helen, eyes glittering with excitement at the coming battle, pointed out to King Priam the mighty warriors she knew. Menelaus himself, Ajax, Agamemnon, Diomedes, Idomeneus, Odysseus. Priam was then escorted down between the armies. Offerings were made to the gods and the oaths were sworn.

Hector and Odysseus measured the ground. The watching armies prayed for an end to war and for their own safe return home.

Hector, turning his eyes away from the helmet held out by Odysseus, drew the lot to decide who would be first to throw his bronze spear. The lot fell to Paris.

The soldiers waited now. Silent.

IV · THE DUEL

Even the sea breeze died. Nothing moved. The armies were still. Paris wore greaves to protect his legs, and a bronze breastplate. His sword had a silver-studded handgrip and his shield a bronze boss at its center. His gilded helmet had a bright-red horsehair crest. Carefully, he chose a spear weighted and balanced for his hand.

Menelaus, who loved to do battle, stood at his mark. The troops sat spellbound as the two men squared up to each other.

The signal was given and the battle began. Paris hurled his long-shadowed spear. It fell, deflected by Menelaus' shield, or perhaps by one of the interfering gods. Menelaus balanced his spear, praying to mighty Zeus to be avenged for Paris' treachery. He hurled his spear with such force that it pierced Paris' shield, tore through his armor, and even ripped the tunic underneath. It drew blood from Paris' thigh. Menelaus followed the hurtling spear into a close attack with his silver-mounted sword. He swung hard against the ridge of Paris' helmet. The sword shattered with the power of the blow and left Menelaus at the mercy of his Trojan opponent.

The soldiers roared both fighters on.

Fast as thought, Menelaus flung himself onto the younger man and grasped the high-maned helmet by its rim. He pulled harder and harder on the helmet, then began to swing his opponent, who choked as the chin strap cut deeper and deeper into his throat.

Menelaus edged back, pulling Paris, who was gasping for air. Menelaus leaned back against the weight of the younger man and twisted the helmet. Paris lost his footing. Mighty Menelaus began to spin as if throwing a discus, still holding the helmet by its rim.

Had it not been for Aphrodite's speed, Paris would surely have been strangled to death. The goddess snapped the leather, and the helmet broke free. Menelaus threw it into the Greek lines, picked up his bronze spear, and once more lunged at Paris. But Aphrodite's favorite had vanished into the dust raised by the struggle. Some say the goddess conjured a mist from the sea to protect Paris. In fact, he hurried back through the Trojan lines and the city gates to his home. Helen turned away, afraid now of her fate.

King Agamemnon proclaimed the Greek hero had won.

"The oaths we made before you all, and the sacrifices to the gods that sanctified those oaths, say that Helen and all her wealth must be given back to us."

The men cheered his words. The High King had spoken.

V · THE BATTLE BEGINS

The gods looked over the armies gathered in front of Troy.

Zeus wondered aloud, "Do we let the Trojans hand Helen back and be done with the battle, or do we stir them up again?"

Hera was furious. "I won't agree to let them hand Helen over. I won't let it be settled so feebly. Paris and the Trojans would get off too lightly. I want war!"

Her demand angered Zeus. "How dare you, Hera, to hate these mortals so much you'd condemn them to suffer more. Is ten years not enough? Friends of yours will die if the war goes on. I shall see to it."

Thunder roared around Mount Olympus and lightning slashed the evening sky as Athena sent word to Pandarus, the Trojan bowman, that mighty Menelaus must die by his hand. Paris and all of Troy would favor him if he broke the truce and killed the Greek hero.

Pandarus bent his bow of curling ibex horn to string it. Then, hidden behind the shields of his friends, he watched Menelaus scanning the

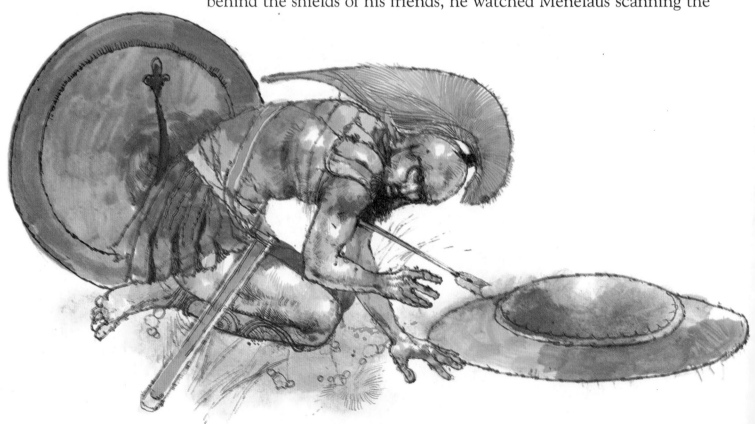

Trojan ranks for Paris. Despite the truce agreed between the leaders of the armies, he nocked his arrow, prayed to the archer god, Apollo, bent the bow in a stiff arc, and fired the humming arrow.

It flew straight at Menelaus and but for a deflection by Athena would have killed the hero. She guided the arrow to the gold buckles of his belt. It pierced his decorated cuirass and leather shirt, then the flesh of his arm. He fell to his knees with the pain. But he did not die.

Agamemnon, seeing his brother wounded, called off the truce. He ordered the Greeks to find the truce-breaker and kill him. And the Trojans, realizing the angry Greeks would strike hard and fast, came on. . . . Again, bloody war would rage.

Agamemnon spurred on his commanders. "Liars and truce-breakers will be left for carrion dogs and vultures to tear apart. We'll take their wives and children as slaves when Troy is burning."

The Greeks cheered and Idomeneus, the Cretan leader, spoke.

"They'll drink death and dishonor, we Cretans swear it."

He saluted the High King. His men unsheathed their swords, checked the arrows in their quivers, and stood ready for the coming battle.

Nestor told his men he regretted he was not young, but promised not to abandon them and to command from his squadron of chariots.

Agamemnon rode on. He found Odysseus and his men waiting behind the front ranks. "Are you afraid of what's coming?" Agamemnon mocked.

Odysseus brusquely told his chief, "You will see our courage when we engage with the Trojans."

Steadily, the Trojan army advanced—chariot wheels rumbling, harnesses clattering, drums thundering, and over all, a cloud of dust. Beyond the battlefield, flocks of long-necked vultures and packs of pariah dogs waited for their feast.

Men were going to die. Helen watched anxiously from the city walls as the warriors surged forward like twin tides about to swallow each other up.

The Greek armies faced the Trojans, their horsehair plumes proudly upright, the relentless sun glinting on metal spears, bosses, and blades.

A shower of death-dealing spears glittered and hissed across the narrowing gap. Men cried out in pain to their gods, their wives, and sons and daughters as they closed their eyes on the world.

The Trojans advanced. Stabbing spearheads emerged through breastbones, throats, and backs. Eyes were sliced by backhand blows of bronze blades. Hurled stones broke noses, shoulders, hipbones . . . and so it went on in ever-mounting chaos.

Echepolus, a Trojan, was the first to die, killed despite his full armor. Darkness came down on his eyes as he fell into the general melee. A friend tried to drag his body clear so it could be taken behind the lines for decent burial. The killer wanted to strip the body of its armor. All around them, swords, stabbing spears, and shield edges crushed and cut and killed.

Ajax struck Anthemion's son, who ended his brief life spitted like a pig through breast and shoulder. A friend attempted to avenge the boy, but, missing Ajax, speared a friend of Odysseus through the groin.

Odysseus, roaring with battle rage, struck and struck again. With the same fury Diomedes, the young Greek, was relentlessly killing elsewhere in the battle.

Apollo tried to rally the Trojans. "These Greeks are only flesh and blood. They don't even have their hero Achilles with them. He's sulking like a woman by the ships. He'll be combing his golden hair."

The Trojans laughed and rallied. But Diomedes was determined to win glory. Athena came to take a hand to balance Apollo's anger. Diomedes used spear and sword to deadly effect. Phegeus the Trojan tried to kill him with his spear, but missed. Diomedes cast and hit his target, tumbling Phegeus from his chariot. Diomedes captured the horses and told his men to take them from the roaring battlefield.

Agamemnon hurled his spear after the Trojan Odius. It hit him in the back, and he fell with a thud under the wheels of his own chariot.

At the same moment, Idomeneus saw the Trojan Phaestus' chariot. With a mighty arm the Cretan flung his spear and took Phaestus under the right shoulder. He crashed the Trojan to the ground. The Cretan's servants stripped the corpse and left it for the dogs.

A mighty chariot raced out of control around the battlefield, its horses driven mad by the stink of blood and the ceaseless roar of battle. The driver lay across the chariot, his bleeding body pinned to the wood by a spear.

The lead horse screamed. An arrow fired by Paris had pierced its skull above the eye.

In the thick of the fighting, the blood-crazed, battle-crazed, insatiable men fought on, killing like machines, unable to stop.

VI · THE BATTLE CONTINUES

Diomedes, inspired by the goddess Athena, found the glory he sought. He seemed to glow with the fire of battle as he tore into the heart of the fight. All over the battlefield, he dealt out death and destruction, taking armor and horses for the Greeks. Men died on the hissing point of his spear, under the terrible chop of his bronze sword blade, or crushed under the wheels of his chariot. He cut a corridor of death as a winter gale cuts down trees. Pandarus, the Trojan truce-breaker, swore to take him out of the battle. Pandarus aimed his bow and hit the edge of Diomedes' breastplate as he pushed into the fray.

Seeing that his arrow had wounded the Greek, Pandarus yelled in triumph, "Come on, Trojans! Forward! Forward, charioteers! Their best man is badly wounded. I, Pandarus, have done it. He won't last long now."

Diomedes held the arrow stuck in his shoulder and called out to his charioteer. "Quick, pull this arrow out. Hurry! Cut it out if you have to."

Quickly it was done. Diomedes, healed by a prayer to Athena, roared back into the battle like the bravest of lions. In the melee of men and swords and horses and flying spears, he found his enemy.

Pandarus threw first and missed. Diomedes cast his deadly spear and hit the Trojan archer on the nose, beside his eye. The spear passed through his teeth, cut off his tongue, and emerged again under his chin. His burnished armor crashed as he fell from his chariot.

His friend, Aeneas, stood over the body to protect it from being stripped of armor. Diomedes flung a huge rock at the spear-carrying Aeneas and crushed his thigh. The world went black for Aeneas, and he would have died if Aphrodite had not rescued him.

The Trojans needed a hero as brave as the bravest Greek. The Greeks were threatening to break through the huge gates into Troy itself.

The god Ares, disguised as Achamas, a hot-blooded ally of the Trojans, demanded to know where the royal princes of the city were hiding.

"Are you going to let these Greeks walk into your city? Are you going to leave your dead and dying to be desecrated by pariah dogs and carrion birds? We need Hector to take on the battle—if he has the courage." Ares, using Achamas' voice, called around the battlefield and mocked the Trojan chief. Others joined in the mockery.

"Come on, Hector," cried one. "Stop using your silver tongue. You'll tell us next you can hold the gates of Troy, just you and your brothers and sisters."

"We don't see one of them here," jeered another.

"Are your allies, who came here over land and sea, to be abandoned in the battle, while you and yours spend your time behind the walls of the city?"

The shouts were angry now.

"You leave us to face these Greeks alone. Get out here and fight!"

There was little time left then before the Trojans' allies would desert and leave the battlefield to the Greeks.

VII · HECTOR

Hector hurtled into the field in full battle armor. His chariot had bronze rails and ivory fittings on the reins. The reins were made of oxhide, strong enough to curb the wildest horses. With his long spear in his left hand, Hector surged through the men fighting hand to hand, just as they were about to retreat.

"Stay!" he called. "You won't fight for nothing. Be real men, not cowards. Don't give another step."

The Trojan forces saw great Hector and his dancing horses searing a path through the Greeks. With sword and spear, Hector stopped the Greek advance almost single-handedly.

All around the battlefield warriors took the armor from the men they had killed: their loot to keep or sell.

When Ajax killed a mighty Trojan, he ran to strip the armor from him, but was kept away by a shower of arrows and swarms of glittering javelins. Ajax quickly planted his foot on the dead man's chest, dragged out his own bronze spear, and retreated.

Hector led the Trojans in a strong assault.

Ajax speared the mighty Achamas, and night came down on Achamas' eyes. Diomedes killed the Trojan Axylus and his chariot driver, sending both to the world below.

The battle surged back and forth, the armies fighting in close and bloody conflict. No quarter was offered or given. If men tried to surrender, they were cut down by merciless blades even as they begged for mercy.

Nestor called out, "No looting now. We are here to kill. So kill. Afterward, you may loot the corpses at your leisure."

The Trojans made their stand near the walls of their city. Hector was urged to return to the city to ask his mother, Hecuba, and his wife, Andromache, to make sacrifice to Athena.

"I'll ask them to pray that Diomedes is never allowed to run amok in our broad streets, for no woman or child would be safe from his bloody sword," he promised. His men cheered.

Hector leapt from his chariot, and as he worked his way back toward the gates, he urged his men on, knowing they needed only to see him to rouse their fighting spirit.

He strode through the ranks of his men, crying out, "My friends, fight with the courage you have always shown. Cover me while I go into the city to make sure our women make proper sacrifice to Athena and the gods of war."

Hector rushed past the women waiting by the gate for news of husbands, sons, and lovers. Ignoring their desperate cries, he hurried into the city. When he reached his mother's house, she offered him wine to pour as an offering to the gods.

Hector refused to make the libation, bespattered as he was with blood and gore. "I cannot pray to Zeus. I am defiled with blood.

You and the women must pray, Mother. Promise Athena a dozen yearlings, cloth, some lambs. Whatever you most value—offer it."

He turned then to try to find his brother Paris.

"He shames us, Mother, and is not worthy of the royal blood. If he were on his way to Hades I would not stop, nor do more than wish him good riddance. No doubt he lies in Helen's arms. But not for much longer, I promise you."

Hector hurried through the empty streets, past the barricaded houses, to Priam's palace. Paris was polishing his shield into a mirror.

Paris looked up in fear as his brother burst in. Helen and her servant were appalled by the blood and filth that covered the mighty warrior from head to foot. They backed away from his rage.

"Get out and fight," Hector ordered.

"I came here," said Paris, "because I felt our warriors mocked me."

"They mock you for your vanity—staring into any mirror you pass. You shame us! They laugh at you for running from Menelaus. Put on your armor. Get outside the walls and run the risks we all run."

"I can't leave Helen," said Paris.

Hector turned away then, but Helen begged him to listen to her.

"I know you think me shameless, and maybe I am, but I have been urging Paris to do his duty."

Hector stared at the lovely woman, and she urged him to rest a moment.

"Not as long as there is fighting to be done and men to lead," Hector replied, turning back to Paris. "I won't wait for you. Come with me to the fighting or I will brand you a coward."

Paris started then in anger, but his brother had already gone to seek out his wife, Andromache, and Scamandrius, his beloved son.

He found Andromache by the Scaean Gate, waiting to embrace her battle-marked man. She had no fear that he would abandon the field. She knew Hector would die there and foretold it.

"When I lose you, dear husband, I too might as well be dead. When you sleep the dark sleep, I will have nothing left in my life."

Andromache knew grief. Had not her father been killed by Achilles? But, it must be said, Achilles treated her father's body honorably. "Achilles freed my mother, but she too is dead now." The noble Andromache looked up into Hector's face and smiled a little. "You are my brother, father, mother, and beloved husband."

Hector held her in his arms and then, gently pushing her away from him, said, "I am not afraid of death, but of what will come of you if these Greeks take our city. I see you as a slave in their land, and whenever you pass, carrying water, men will say, 'There goes Hector's wife.' I will lie deep in the earth before I hear the screams you make when they carry you away."

Hector leaned down and kissed his son. He and the child's mother saw that the boy was afraid of his bloody, battle-weary father.

Holding the child, Hector prayed to Zeus.

"May people say, when this child comes back from battle, that he is a better man than his father."

Hector hugged his child again and kissed his wife. He begged her not to weep, and walked away after saying to her that he knew he would not die until Fate said it was time.

"Go home now, Andromache, pray and attend to the loom, for that is your work. War is men's work, and this war is above all the work of Trojans and of your husband."

He replaced his helmet, then saw Paris hurrying to join him. Together, the brothers went through the high gates of Troy with one purpose—to drive the Greeks from Trojan soil.

VIII · CHAMPIONS MEET

The gods looked down from Mount Olympus. Athena was anxious that the Trojan forces would wreak havoc among her favorites, who were led by Agamemnon. She hurried down to aid the Greeks.

Apollo, who favored the Trojans, raced to intercept her. They met near the roaring battlefield, and in the din of the battle the two schemers talked.

"I know what you want, Athena," said Apollo. "You want nothing more or less than Troy of the broad streets burned to ashes."

Athena tried to interrupt, but Apollo went on. "It's late afternoon. The sun will set in an hour. I will persuade Hector to challenge the Greeks to send a hero to fight him in a duel."

Athena laughed at that.

"I hope for your sake he's braver than his brother."

"We'll see," said Apollo.

Athena and Apollo sat in a huge oak tree, leaned their weapons against the uppermost branches, and waited. During a lull in the fighting, Hector stepped in front of the Trojan lines, holding back his own men with his shield and spear. Then he stepped into the no-man's-land between the armies to issue his challenge.

"It seems that Zeus, from his high throne, wants to watch us suffer until you bring down the towers of Troy or until you are beaten back to the beaches and into your ships. I propose we end this gory battle and that I fight your champion man to man—winner take all."

The Greeks sat in the dust to rest their bruised and bloody bodies, as the Trojans did: rank after rank of men, weapons ready by their sides, spears upright like a porcupine's protective quills.

Hector spoke as the two armies listened silently.

"As Zeus is my witness, if your man wins, he may strip my armor and take it, but he must leave my body so that my wife and the Trojans may burn it properly. If Apollo lets me win, I promise that your man may be buried and a mound raised to make a monument to a warrior killed in single combat by the heroic Hector. Choose a champion to fight me."

No one moved. Hector looked slowly along the lines of Greek soldiers, but none would meet the eye of this fearless man.

Apollo looked at Athena and smirked. They watched from the top branches of the oak—two bent-necked vultures waiting, waiting.

Eventually, there was a flurry of movement, and a man stood up. It was Menelaus, who cried to the men around him, "You women of Greece—sit there and rot! I will fight Hector myself."

Menelaus began to prepare his most glorious armor, though he knew he was as good as dead. Hector was by far a greater fighter than he.

The Greeks needed mighty Achilles, but he sat in the shade by his ships and slept.

Agamemnon hurried to his brother and begged Menelaus not to fight. "Brother, even Achilles is afraid to meet Hector in single combat. Go and sit down. We will find another to fight this man."

Reluctantly, Menelaus gave way and sat apart from the other men, ashamed.

Apollo shifted on his branch and lifted his long and scraggy neck to the bright sun. Athena sat and waited. Below them, Nestor, the old and wise, rose to his feet to speak.

"It's enough to make the whole of Greece weep. How the great heroes of our past would be shamed, as I am shamed. If I were younger I would stand. But words are easy, as you cowards know."

He went on angrily until nine men could bear it no longer. Diomedes, Idomeneus and his squire, and six others claimed the right to fight.

"You will choose by lot," said Nestor, and each man made his mark on a stone and tossed it into Nestor's helmet.

The lot that came to Nestor's hand when he took the burnished helmet was what they all had wished for. Ajax rejoiced. He turned and asked them to pray to Zeus for his victory.

In the tree, Apollo watched eagerly. Athena was relieved that the Greeks had a man willing to fight the mighty Hector.

Ajax adjusted his flashing bronze armor—the bright metal buckled to his legs and the burnished metal on his shoulders and down his back, carved and etched with images of wild animals and the goddess Athena. His sword blade was inlaid with gold and silver, his helmet topped with a curving mane of horsehair dyed blood-red. He took his spear and his seven-layered oxhide shield and stepped into no-man's-land.

"Now," he said to Hector, "you will see what kind of men we Greeks are, even when the best of us, Achilles, the Breaker of Men, lies by his ships. You will see."

Hector answered Ajax as a brave man would—without boasting.

"I know, Prince Ajax, who you are, and you cannot frighten me with words. I am a fighter. At a distance or hand to hand, I am ready. But let me say I see a man before me. So, let's fight!"

With that, Hector flung his dark-shadowed javelin. It tore through six layers of Ajax's shield; the seventh held. Ajax flung his javelin. It glanced off the shining boss of Hector's shield, sliced through the leather tunic over his thigh, but missed his flesh as Hector swerved aside.

Now they fell on each other like savage beasts. Ajax cut Hector's neck with a spear blow. Hector drew back a little,

bent over, and in one movement took up and hurled a jagged rock at Ajax. His shield rang out as the stone hit the boss. Ajax quickly hurled a boulder that swept Hector off his feet and smashed his shield.

Apollo saw that his hero about to be butchered by Ajax and raised his man to his feet.

Athena was angry, but it was too late.

Again, the two men fell on each other, this time with broad-bladed swords flashing in the evening light. Back and forth they fought, sometimes hidden in the clouds of whirling dust they raised. Often, all the armies knew were the clashing sounds of bronze on bronze and of grunts as the two men slashed and parried, hit and thrust.

The sun began to fall beyond the sea, and dark shadows stretched over the battleground. The shadows of long spears fell across the dust.

In a pause, as the champions dragged in breath to slow their pumping hearts, Hector said, "Ajax, you are a worthy champion and a great spearman. I admit it. But the light is fading. If I suggest we stop fighting today, we can meet again and go on until the gods decide which of us shall die."

With blood smearing their arms, their necks, and their chests, the two men looked into each other's eyes and trusted what they saw.

Ajax pushed his blunted sword into its sheath.

Hector, to the surprise of his men, unfastened his sword belt and handed it with his silver-studded sword to his opponent. Ajax took off his own splendid purple belt and handed it to Hector.

The two men clasped hands and parted friends.

The sun fell over the rim of the world. Night.

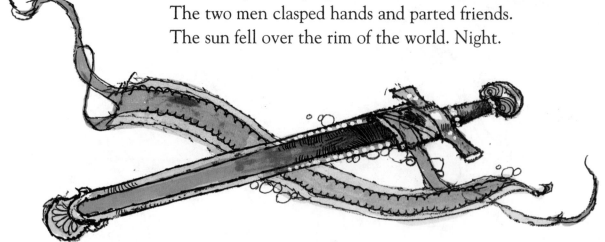

IX · Burials

Along the walls of Troy, sentries kept watch over the plain above the beaches and the shadows of the Greek ships.

Small fires glinted across the plain and down to the sea as the Greek warriors cleaned their weapons, repaired their dented armor, and cooked their rations of meat and bread. Soon they would pour a little wine from their wineskins onto the earth as libations to Zeus, the father of the gods. After drinking they would lie under the black sky and the shimmering points of starlight, and sleep.

In Agamemnon's hut, the chieftains honored the bravery of Ajax. The High King served him his food first and poured the first wine for him to make a suitable offering to the gods, so that the warriors could then eat and drink.

Nestor, the wise man, stood and asked to speak; the others fell into respectful silence.

"I suggest we offer a truce to the Trojans so that we can collect our dead. They will want to do the same. Then we may burn our friends and collect their bones to take back to their sons and wives. At the same time we should build a line of defense to protect our ships. I suggest a deep ditch and a wooden and stone wall with gates wide enough to allow our war chariots through."

The Greeks agreed.

Meanwhile, on the silent streets inside Troy's walls, nothing moved. But in King Priam's palace, men and women were gathered to honor Hector for his courage.

One man turned the celebration sour. Antenor stood and suggested that it was time to bring the war to an end.

"Helen should be given back, together with all the treasure Paris brought from Sparta. That was our promise when Menelaus stood in combat against Paris and beat him. Not to do so dishonors us."

Paris, naturally, was against the idea. He reluctantly offered to pay back all he had taken when he left Sparta with Helen, wife of Menelaus. But Helen he would not return.

Priam felt that was as much as anyone could expect and suggested they send a messenger to King Agamemnon to see if he would agree. They could also suggest to the Greeks that they be allowed to collect their dead before the fighting was resumed. King Priam's men agreed.

The next morning the Greeks welcomed a truce, but refused to accept Paris' offer unless Helen was also returned to them. So, as the sun rose, spraying golden light across the hills and down toward the Greek ships, small groups of men could be seen spreading out from the gates of Troy and up from the beaches and ships of the Greeks.

Carefully, the Greeks collected the bodies of their friends and washed them. They gathered sticks, branches, and driftwood into huge piles. Onto these they gently laid the bodies with their armor and offerings of food and wine.

Soon the Trojans on the walls and the guards on the beach saw coils of pale smoke rising from countless pyres. It was a desolate business.

Meanwhile, the Greeks had done as Nestor suggested and built a defensive wall across the approaches to the beach to protect their ships.

Zeus, Lord of Lightning, looked down from Olympus as the Greeks built their wall. Poseidon, the Earthshaker, watching with him, was angry.

"They haven't asked us. They haven't poured libations. They haven't prayed, or sacrificed so much as a herring. And that wall is a huge work that will be famous—more famous even than walls Apollo and I have built," Poseidon grumbled.

Zeus laughed. "Don't worry about your memorials, old Earthshaker. You will always be famous. A single storm will blow away their work. You can see to that. And tomorrow they'll be at each other's throats again for our amusement."

Small groups of men in the killing zone worked to untangle friends' bodies locked in death with enemy bodies. They kicked away the carrion birds already pecking at the eyes and spilled entrails, and carried the mangled remains to the pyres. They honored their dead friends and sent them quietly to Hades. The sun set again, and to the sentries watching from the high walls of Troy it seemed as if the smoldering, sputtering flames of five thousand funeral pyres were reflected in the stars.

Across the dark sky, lightning flickered and thunder rolled in a neverending warning.

Zeus was restless.

X · TO BATTLE AGAIN

It was early. The sun glinted palely across the dry dust of the plain, glittered on the edge of the sea. The two armies prepared to fight again. On Olympus, Zeus was not in the best of tempers. He called a meeting of the gods, determined that none should meddle in the battle but him.

The other gods listened in fear, trembling as his words thundered around the mountaintops.

"Anyone who disobeys me—" He looked sharply at his wife, Hera, and at Athena and Apollo. "Anyone who dares even to think about helping Trojans or Greeks, I will hurl into the deepest yawning chasm of Tartarus. No one will interfere in this battle—not even if their favorite is being butchered. Do you hear me, Aphrodite?"

The shining goddess nodded, for once unable to speak for fear of Zeus.

"If anyone defies me, I will take Earth and Heaven and Sea and hang them all over the darkest chasm, and leave them—and you—dangling."

At last, Athena found her tongue. "Father Zeus, we are sorry for the terrible fate of the armies below."

The gods could see the Greek army standing ready in the killing field. Rushing out of the Trojan gates came war chariots and as many men as there are stubble spears after harvest.

Zeus let loose a thunderclap, and battle was joined. First, the slashing hiss of volleys of arrows, followed by the clatter of hurled javelins as they were deflected off shield and breastplate, and thuds as they crashed into throats and breasts and skulls. Desperate sounds of sword on bronze, sword on bone, and piercing, terrible cries of dying men filled the air in an endless roar as if the earth itself were an animal crying in terror over the world.

Back and forth the battle raged.

Diomedes was nearly killed when Hector attacked. He was forced to run, and Hector shouted abuse after the Greek.

Zeus flung a bolt of lightning that burned the ground and flayed all it touched. It terrified the Greeks, who believed it was a sure sign that Zeus was with the Trojan forces.

Hera begged Poseidon to do something to curb the Trojans, but even the Lord of Earthquake dared not defy Zeus.

The Greeks were forced back. It was a chaos of death in the deep ditch they had dug in front of their wall.

Agamemnon called on the Greeks to rally. Privately, he begged Zeus not to let them die in this trap of their own making. Zeus was moved and sent a sign. An eagle flew over the nearby hillside with a fawn in its claws. The huge bird climbed higher over the battlefield until it was over the Greeks. Then it dropped the fawn. The Greeks saw this as a sign that Zeus had changed his mind and threw themselves against their enemy with all the joy of battle.

XI · ZEUS'S MESSAGE

Achilles sat on the sand by the Greek ships and played dice with his warriors. He ignored the distant sound of the roaring battle.

Ajax had a partner in battle, a bowman named Teucer. Ajax would shield him as he prepared his curved-horn bow, then move his shield aside for Teucer to find his target. Instantly, an arrow hissed home to some Trojan throat, eye, or brain.

They searched for Hector, the bravest Trojan in the field. Then Teucer saw him in the thick of battle. He bent his bow and aimed. His first arrow killed one of Priam's younger sons; the second killed Hector's charioteer.

Hector called another to take the reins and leapt to the ground. Picking up a lump of rock, he headed straight for Teucer, who had left the protection of Ajax's shield. Teucer was taking aim as Hector threw the jagged stone. It struck the archer's shoulder, numbing his arm. Hector moved in for the kill, but Ajax covered Teucer with his mighty shield. Two Greeks lifted the groaning bowman and carried him out of danger.

High on Olympus, the goddesses wept for the Greeks, who were being hurled back again. Hector ordered the Trojans to set fire to the ships when they reached them. Without their ships, the Greeks would be stranded.

Hera and Athena begged Zeus to give the Greeks a chance.

Zeus sent a message from where he lay resting as the sun set across the wine-dark sea. "Those goddesses know what will happen if they even think of interfering. Tell them," he told his messenger, "Hector will harass his enemies until Achilles fights. And that will not be until the Trojans are closing in on the ships, carrying burning torches. The Greeks will fight to protect Patroclus, Achilles' friend, who is not yet dead. Then, and only then, will Achilles join the battle."

The sun set crimson over the black sea. The Trojans withdrew, to the great relief of the Greeks, who had been longing for the sun to leave the sky. It vanished just in time.

XII · AN APOLOGY

It was cold on the beaches when the sun fell into the sea. The Greeks huddled behind their wall. They could smell meat cooking on the Trojan fires just beyond their defenses. They were afraid.

Agamemnon walked along the beach, touched his tall ships, prayed to Zeus, and decided to call together the war council. When they had gathered, he lifted his powerful head, and they saw tears in his eyes.

"Ten years ago," he said, "I told you that Zeus promised me we would destroy the mighty towers of Troy and bring back Helen with a thousand Trojan women. He has abandoned me."

The chiefs were appalled as Agamemnon went on, "I believe we must launch our ships for home. Troy will never fall to us." He looked away from their accusing eyes. They knew he was testing them this time.

Diomedes stood and said what the others felt. "I blame you. Your stupid quarrel with Achilles over a woman lost us that great fighter. You accused others of cowardice. You should have set an example. Courage is the secret of power.

"Zeus may have given you the imperial scepter and the homage due to it," he went on, "but he didn't give you courage. If you want to go . . . go! If anyone else wants to go with you, then I say go! I'll stay and fight—alone if I have to. We shall win. The gods will it."

As the men applauded Diomedes, Nestor the Wise rose to speak.

"Agamemnon, son of Atreus, King of Men," he said formally. "Zeus made you High King of a great people. You must remember not only to give advice, but also to listen to it."

Nestor looked around him, and all present hung on his words.

"You must bring Achilles back into the fold. Apologize to him."

There was a long pause.

Agamemnon slowly lifted his head and looked at the circle of silent men. The fire cast flickering shadows over their battle-weary faces.

Agamemnon, King of Men, bowed his head.

"I will do it," he said. "And I will give him great gifts. When we are home, he can choose a wife from my three daughters. Briseis will be sent back to him. She has not been touched since she has been in my camp. Send messengers to ask Achilles if he will hear me."

He sat down among the chiefs as they chose the envoys to make the offer to Achilles. Ajax was to go with Odysseus, the old fox, to whom the chiefs thought Achilles might listen most favorably.

While the envoys set out along the foreshore to Achilles' encampment, Nestor and Diomedes sent sentries to guard the walls and ditch that kept the Trojans at bay.

A bright moon reflected silver over the calm waters of the sea.

As Ajax and Odysseus approached Achilles' hut, they heard the sound of a silver lyre. As the two envoys entered the hut, they were confronted by Patroclus, who sat listening to his friend. Achilles stopped playing and stood politely for the two older men.

"You are welcome, Lords Odysseus and Ajax. I have heard, Lord Ajax, that you were magnificent in combat against the mighty Hector. And also, Lord Odysseus, that you sent many a Trojan into the night that never ends. Please sit and eat."

The men drank wine together. Achilles knew why the two men had come, but he gave no sign. They ate grilled meat brought to them by Patroclus, and eventually, Odysseus judged the time was right.

"My lord—" he began as Achilles also spoke. "Odysseus—"

Both men stopped and smiled, and Achilles politely indicated that Odysseus should speak first.

"We face disaster. The Trojans are at our walls, threatening destruction. Zeus favors them. Hector has run berserk through our army and fears no one. He waits impatiently for the dawn so he can send our ships up in flames and slaughter us all by their charred hulls. There is no mercy shown. None.

"Your father was my dear friend," Odysseus went on. Achilles sat silent. "I know he told you that the goddesses Athena and Hera would make you strong. Keep a check on your pride, and remember kindness is best. We need you. We Greeks need the mighty Achilles. And Agamemnon admits his fault to you."

Odysseus and Ajax told the silent Achilles of the gifts Agamemnon had promised. They begged him to accept the gifts and fight with them.

"If you can't forgive Agamemnon the wrongs he has done, then pity our warriors, who are exhausted and face tomorrow with fear in their hearts," Ajax pleaded with the silent man.

Odysseus offered him temptation.

"Hector yells across no-man's-land that there is no Greek to match him. No one who can beat him. Maybe that's the truth," said the old fox silkily.

Achilles looked up, and for a moment Odysseus thought he had hooked his man. But Achilles shook his head.

"Odysseus, I struggled day in and day out, year in and year out, and got no thanks from Agamemnon. Then he took my prize. He pretends to be brave, but rewards the cowards. We have fought hard, mighty Ajax—and you too, Odysseus, who knew my father. I do not respect Agamemnon. We are here to take home Helen, wife of Menelaus. Maybe Menelaus loves Helen. Maybe Helen loves Paris. I *know* I love

Briseis. Agamemnon took her and gives her back untouched, and no doubt will take her again if he chooses, because he is High King. I will not fight for him."

Odysseus tried to persuade the younger man.

Achilles shook his head sadly. "When I was fighting, no Trojan came within a bowshot of our ships. Now they sit outside the walls and wait for morning light. Then they will fall on the ships with blazing torches. So be it. Tomorrow, I will load my ships, make an offering to Zeus, and leave.

"At dawn, look out to sea, and you will see my men at their oars and the fish dancing in the water beside us. Tell your king that I will take my prizes—all save Briseis, whom I love more than gold, silver, iron, or bronze, but *not* more than my honor, which has been insulted. Tell him in front of the other chiefs—and don't come again.

"Agamemnon is mad, jealous, and grasping, and has his reward. As for his gifts, I like them as little as I like the man. I would not have any daughter of

his as my wife, even if she were as lovely as Aphrodite or clever as Athena. No thank you—not for me."

The envoys gathered their cloaks as Achilles finished speaking and walked slowly to the door of the hut. Before they stepped into the darkness, he added quietly, "I honor you, Ajax, for your courage, and you, my Lord Odysseus, for your cunning. I believe Zeus will not let Troy be taken. So I suggest you, too, sail for home on the morning tide."

The envoys waited. He went on, "I swear this. Even if I stay, I will not think of battle unless Prince Hector, son of wise Priam, reaches my warriors' ships. If he tries to torch my black ships, Hector may find himself stopped."

Odysseus and Ajax walked away from Achilles' ships, which lay close enough to the water for it to lap against the hulls. Both men were disappointed by their failure to change Achilles' mind. They took his message to Agamemnon's hut, where the chieftains waited. Odysseus told them bluntly and left them appalled and angry.

"My Lord," said Diomedes, "you have fed his pride by making your offer. He's a stiff-necked man. We must be ready for the attack that is surely coming at dawn. I suggest we try to sleep."

They stepped out into the moonlight. All around them lay the shapes of warriors lying under blankets and lion skins, sleeping.

XIII · AMBUSH

It was not yet dawn. Sleeping soldiers lay scattered across the cool sand, each with shield and weapons ready for instant action should the Trojans spring a surprise attack.

Agamemnon paced the camp with his brother, Menelaus. They met Nestor, who had been checking that the sentries were alert for any sign of a Trojan raid. An experienced soldier, Nestor carried a strong spear with a bronze head and wore a thick, purple cloak against the cold.

Agamemnon confessed his concern about the coming battle. He still believed they should retreat in their boats. The three men went to rouse the senior officers.

Diomedes slept outside, surrounded by his men, their spears stuck upright in the sand close to their hands. Nestor touched the sleeping man's foot.

"Wake up. Why should you sleep while old men keep guard?"

Nestor smiled fondly at the brave Diomedes, who picked up his spear and a lion skin that reached from his shoulders to his heels.

Beyond them in the dark, the war dogs yelped, then were silent.

Nestor suggested it would help to know what the Trojans had planned for the morning. If someone could pass through their lines, they might hear something, or bring back a prisoner for questioning.

Diomedes volunteered at once and asked Odysseus to be his companion. Odysseus, who loved adventure, agreed.

Diomedes borrowed a double-edged sword. He wore an oxhide cap and carried a shield. Odysseus was given a bow, a quiver full of arrows, and a sword. His helmet was leather with a soft cap under it. The rim was covered with a row of white boar's tusks.

As the two men slipped away from the Greek camp, they heard a nervous squawk from a heron in the marshland.

"Athena sends us a sign, my friend," said the older man, and he prayed for their safe return with some useful information. Then they slipped into the no-man's-land between the mighty forces and stopped to catch their breath.

On the other side, behind the Trojan lines, Dolon, a vain man, had volunteered to cross into the Greek lines to seek out some weakness in the Greek defenses. He boasted his intention to go as far as Agamemnon's ship. He had chosen to go alone, as he wanted all the glory and reward for himself. He made Hector promise that he would have Achilles' horses and fabulously decorated chariot as his reward. Hector swore by Zeus that he would have both.

Dolon slipped through the Trojan camp and into the treacherous no-man's-land, wearing a gray wolf skin and with an ermine-skin cap on his head. He hurried once he was clear of Trojan lines.

Odysseus and Diomedes saw the gray figure scurrying toward them. They let him pass, then turned to hurry after him. Dolon thought that they were friends coming to join him, or that perhaps Hector had changed his mind and wanted him to return to the camp.

A dark cloud slid aside from the pale moon.

In that moment, Dolon saw that the two men were enemies. He turned and ran. But fleet-footed Diomedes gave chase, and as the distance between them shortened, he let fly his spear, deliberately missing Dolon.

Terrified, Dolon stopped.

Odysseus and Diomedes took the weeping man by his arms. He begged them to take him alive. He promised gold, which his father would pay if they let him live.

Odysseus urged Dolon not to think of dying. They only wanted to know whether Hector had sent him—and if so, why? Or had he decided to come for his own reasons?

Dolon, shaking with fear, told them Hector had persuaded him to come by promising him Achilles' horses and chariot. "Hector wanted to know if the ships are guarded and if the men are thinking about running away."

The two men terrified the Trojan spy. They asked about sentries and passwords. Dolon told them all.

Diomedes hid his sword behind his back.

Odysseus pulled the frightened man into the shadow of an old tree and, smiling still, asked him quietly where Hector was, and did he have his armor near him?

"Are his horses close by and ready? Do they plan to hold their advanced position by the ships or to go back to the city after they have defeated the Greeks? Just answer us truthfully, my friend," whispered the cunning fox.

And Dolon did. Odysseus asked him for the positions of all the most important warriors in the Trojan army and where their horses were, and their spears and bows.

In fear for his life, Dolan spilled out everything. "And there are two of the loveliest horses I have ever seen, owned by Rhesus, King of Thrace. He sleeps beside them and his glorious chariot near the front line, over to the right. The horses are snow white, and the chariot is decorated with gold and ivory."

The two Greeks smiled at each other at this news.

Dolon went on, "I have been truthful, as I said I would. Now take me hostage back to your lines. I won't make a sound."

Diomedes looked down at the miserable man, who had bent to clasp his knees in submission. He took his double-edged sword from behind his back and slashed the Trojan's head from his neck. Dolon was dead before he had stopped speaking.

The two Greeks moved behind the Trojan lines. Near a group of sleeping men, they found the two white horses belonging to King Rhesus. Odysseus killed three guards and a charioteer, then fastened the nervous horses to Rhesus' own chariot.

Meanwhile, Diomedes silently slaughtered twelve more sleeping Trojans.

Odysseus whistled as soon as the horses were harnessed. Diomedes mounted the chariot. Odysseus drove like wind through the Trojan encampment to safety beyond the Greek front line.

Their arrival with the wonderful horses, and the news that they had killed seventeen Trojans and were not even scratched, lifted the spirits of the Greeks.

While the horses were rubbed down, fed, and watered, Odysseus and Diomedes went into the sea and washed the sweat and blood from their bodies, rubbed themselves with olive oil, and then made suitable libations to the goddess Athena.

The archer god, Apollo, raged with fury.

Dawn broke over the silver sea, capping the looming gate towers of Troy with sunlight. The keen-eyed could see women on the walls, looking out over the plain for signs of husbands, sons, and lovers.

The Trojan warriors were still in shadow as the sun glinted on the high, vaulting prows of the Greek fleet, passed over the eyes painted on them—yellow, red, and black—and touched the spears still upright in the sand. The Greeks were ready, like hounds about to be unleashed.

Agamemnon stood before them, eager for battle. His red-crested helmet sparkled in the yellow morning light. His breastplate flashed with strips of dark-blue enamel, gold, and bronze; three snakes coiled up to the neck. Gold studs glittered on his sword, and the Gorgon-faced boss on his shield reflected the light in dazzling lines into the eager faces of his men, and up to the distant sky where Hera and Athena saluted.

The Greek warriors awaited their leader's order.

They waited and waited. . . .

Beyond the Greeks' ditch, the Trojans fell in under their captains. The young and glorious Achamas, Aeneas, Agenor, and Polydamus gathered around the great Hector. He walked into the thick of the army, encouraging his warriors. They would burn the Greek fleet where it stood and slaughter the soldiers without mercy. It was about to begin.

Agamemnon looked across his armies, and Nestor lifted his spear in salute. Odysseus lifted his sword. Diomedes and Ajax waited . . . straining for the word so they would be first into battle.

Agamemnon raised his spear and roared, "WARRRRRRR!"

The wild warriors poured over the ditch like a roaring spring tide. They had no distance to charge before they were in the thick of it.

Through the morning and into the heat of midday the battle raged. It was grim, unyielding, violent work.

On the beach Achilles heard, but turned away and struck another chord on his silver lyre.

Chariots thundered across the open spaces; horses were hamstrung or crazed by the noise and blood. Hector and other fighters left their chariots to fight on foot—hand to hand, blade to blade.

Blood soaked the sand beneath their feet. Bodies were trampled or thrown aside, the armor stripped from them. Arms and legs grew wounds like flowers, shoulders were smashed, faces opened by slicing sword or crunching spear. This was WAR!

Agamemnon did his share of slaughter, sent looted armor back to his chariot, then sought more Trojan heroes to send to the neverending dark.

Greeks and Trojans fell like corn under the scythe. Yet on they came. For each who died, another stepped into his place.

Zeus looked down from where he sat on Mount Ida and saw Troy and the Greek ships, and the shimmering wave of men and bronze and blood pouring at the feet of the warriors.

Hector rallied his men and sent his share of Greeks to eternal dark. This was WAR!

Two brothers begged Agamemnon for mercy, but he struck Peisander on the breast with his spear and flung him from his chariot.

Hippolochus leapt down to
defend his brother. Agamemnon slashed his head and
arms from his body and moved on.

This was WAR!

Empty chariots, drawn by fear-crazed horses, raced in deadly
circles among the fighting men. The Greeks swept eagerly over the
plain toward the city walls.

Agamemnon led his men to the gates of the city.

Zeus, seeing this, called for Iris, his messenger. "Tell Hector that when
he sees Agamemnon taken away from the battlefield in his chariot, that
is the time to counterattack. I, Zeus, will give him the strength to take
his men as far as the Greek ships, and then the sun will set."

Hector, encouraged, urged his men to stand and hold the Greeks.

Agamemnon charged at the Trojans. He found himself confronted by
Iphidamas of Thrace. Iphidamas lunged forward and thrust his spear under
the High King's cuirass. He leaned his weight on the shaft, but he could not
slice through the belt.

Agamemnon pulled both shaft and man toward him, dragged the spear from his hand, and stabbed down. Iphidamas fell, pinned by the throat as he went to endless darkness.

Agamemnon was pulling the armor off the body when Coon, the dead man's brother, struck. His spearpoint pierced the High King's forearm. As Coon tried to pull Iphidamas away, Agamemnon struck upward and killed him. Then, even as his arm poured blood, he took the armor off both men and looked for his chariot.

The charioteer came close enough for Agamemnon to hurl himself into it and be taken from the battle to the surgeons behind the lines.

Hector, remembering Zeus's words, ordered his men to fight harder now the Greek High King was gone. The Trojans came on, snarling like hounds. The Greeks, like wild boars bloody and hunched in a dark forest, were forced to retreat. Hector came on, cutting into their ranks.

The Greeks turned to run, and the Trojans fell on them in waves.

Diomedes was wounded and taken behind the Greek lines, and even Machaon, the great healer, was wounded by an arrow fired by Paris. Machaon, friend of Achilles, was hurried off in Nestor's chariot to be treated. He was too valuable a healer for the Greeks to lose.

Odysseus fought on like the lion he was. Using his spear as sword and chopper, he took down men like a woodsman felling saplings. Ennomus and Chersidamas both fell and clutched the earth. Charops, another Trojan, shut his eyes on the day. Socos boasted he would kill Odysseus and wounded him with a hurtling spear. Odysseus speared Socos between his shoulders—its point came out through the Trojan's chest.

As Odysseus, standing on the back of the dead man, pulled out his spear, he too was bleeding from his wound.

"Help me!" he cried to his friends. "Cover me. Help!"

Trojans went in for the kill, but Ajax and Menelaus went to Odysseus' aid and covered the old fox. When the Trojans saw who was protecting him, they scattered to seek easier prey. Leaning against Menelaus, Odysseus was helped into his chariot and driven away to be treated.

On the other wing, the Trojans were being forced back until Hector hurried to join them in the thick of the fight.

Trojans and Greeks were trampling on corpses. Chariot wheels and axles were sprayed with the blood thrown by the iron-grooved wheels. Hector saw Ajax defending the wounded Odysseus, but avoided him.

Ajax, looking up from the battle, saw he was heavily outnumbered and slowly retreated, checking all the time for danger, turning at bay sometimes to give himself and his men time to reach the Greek defenses.

Eurypylus, King of Cos, seeing Ajax in danger, let loose his javelin and struck the Trojan who was about to attack mighty Ajax. Even as the javelin flew, Paris bent his bow and hit Eurypylus with an arrow. Eurypylus took cover with his men, the arrow still sticking out of his thigh.

Behind the lines, Nestor's chariot raced toward the ships and huts of the Greeks, carrying wounded men, including the healer Machaon. It passed the ship from which Achilles was watching the desperate battle. He looked down and saw his bleeding friend pass by in a chariot of wounded.

Machaon was laid down gently and his wound treated and bound by his own instruction.

Suddenly, at the door of the hut, Patroclus, Achilles' friend, appeared. Nestor looked around at him irritably.

"What do you want with us?" he asked. "We're busy here."

"I have to see how badly Machaon has been wounded. Achilles wants to know. I must hurry, for Achilles is an impatient man."

"I don't understand why he's concerned with a single casualty when the whole of the army suffers. Diomedes, Odysseus, Agamemnon are all wounded, and Eurypylus still has an arrow in his thigh. Achilles has a strange way of showing his concern. Is he waiting until all our ships are in flames and we are butchered to a man? I wish I were still young, sir—I'd show Achilles the meaning of courage."

And the old man turned away from Patroclus, adding, "If you want to help, persuade your master to let you go into battle in his armor with the hordes he brought, instead of letting them play games on the beach. You'd bring fresh blood to the fight, and we might push the Trojans back."

"I will try," said Patroclus.

He ran from the hut and along the beach. On his way he passed Odysseus' ships. Sitting there was Eurypylus, the arrow stuck deep into his thigh. Moved by his bravery, Patroclus knelt on the sand beside the sweating man and asked, "Is there any hope we shall hold Hector, or will we be destroyed where we stand?"

Eurypylus shook his head. "All our heroes are wounded, the enemy grows stronger. There is no hope."

Patroclus sighed and moved to go.

"Before you go and tell Achilles that he could turn the day, help me. Cut out this arrow, wash the wound, and see me safe on my ship. I know you can heal me, for you have learned the art from Achilles, who learned it from Cheiron the Centaur."

Patroclus took his sharp knife, gave Eurypylus a sword hilt to bite on, then cut into the flesh and took the three-barbed arrow from his thigh.

Above them on the plain the noise of battle roared on.

XV · OMENS

Desperate men do desperate things. So it is in war.

The Trojans, determined to reach the ships on the other side of the ditch, pushed forward, but were held at bay by Ajax and Idomeneus. Behind them, the Greeks desperately reorganized.

The ditch was too wide for chariots to cross. Horses balked when they came to the edge. The Greeks had pounded in sharpened stakes to make the crossing even more difficult.

From behind the palisade the Greeks kept up an unending shower of arrows and stones. Bowmen shot, too, from the Trojan side, and the palisade was filled with arrows, like a porcupine with its quills clattering defiance.

Each side rained stones in flurries on their enemies. Their clatter and thunder on helmets and shields was deafening.

The Greeks had to hold. To retreat now would be to allow the Trojans onto the beach and among their ships.

The Trojans raised their shields, charged, and were repulsed again and again.

Hector and Polydamus formed a raiding party of the bravest Trojans. As they prepared to leap down into the ditch, they heard a cry from the men behind them.

Flying along their lines, high in the sky, an eagle struggled to hold on to something in its cruel claws.

As it flew closer, the men saw that the eagle held a huge, blood-red snake. The eagle's wings swung up for balance as it struck down at the writhing beast. As the eagle struck, so did the snake, fixing its fangs in the eagle's neck.

In agony, the huge bird released the snake. It dropped among the Trojans as the eagle, screaming in pain, flew away on an eddy of wind.

"Zeus is sending us a warning. . . . Zeus is turning against us. . . . The Thundermaker is on the Greek side," the men whispered fearfully as the snake writhed on the ground.

"I'm not interested in birds and snakes and so-called omens. Zeus the Thunderer has promised victory, and he is with *us*," Hector said, ordering the company back into battle.

At first it did seem that Zeus was still on Hector's side. He raised a wind that blew sand and dust into the faces of the Greeks as they tried to repulse the charging Trojans. Yet still the Greek defenses held.

It was the Trojan Sarpedon who showed where to make the fatal breach, by racing across the ditch and scaling the mounds of boulders that formed the base of the wall. He was followed by men determined to force back the Greek defenders.

The noise was as loud as a winter avalanche in the mountains of Crete. The defenders called on Ajax for support. He and Teucer, the bowman, began to pick off the warriors who had followed Hector across the ditch to the base of the wall. Teucer cut down men with his arrows, and Ajax smashed men's skulls and hipbones with huge boulders thrown from the top of the wall.

Yet slowly and surely the Trojans began to gain a foothold.

Along the battlements the stones were soaked with Trojan and Greek blood. It was Zeus who tipped the balance for the Trojans, and Hector yelled to his foot soldiers to tear down the huge Greek gates.

Hector leaned down to pick up a boulder no man could lift. Zeus gave him the strength. He lifted and threw. . . .

The gates ripped from their hinges, shattered by the force of the boulder. The breach filled with a chaos of men and weapons.

Hector, gripping two spears, raced for the gap with a look like nightfall. He and his men brought panic to the Greeks. They fled between their curving ships.

Hell was loose on the beaches.

XVI · Interfering Gods

Hand to desperate hand, the Greeks fought. Step by bloody step, the Trojans advanced over the treacherous sand. Slowly, they edged toward the wooden hulls of the swan-necked ships. The smoke and flames swirling from their blazing brands came closer.

The ships reared up on the beach, propped upright by poles, as they had been since the fleet arrived. Their masts and oars were safely stowed over the piles of loot the Greek army had taken.

Hector called, "Come on, Trojans, we'll burn these ships without the help of signs and portents from the gods. That blood-red snake was no warning from Zeus." His men believed him as he strode magnificently into the thick of the battle.

Poseidon, who favored the Greeks, rose through the waves and watched the battle from a mountaintop in Samothrace. He was angry when Zeus gave all his aid to the Trojan forces. He moved down the mountainside, making the forests tremble as he swept toward the sea. He harnessed his fastest horses to his chariot and drove out over the waves.

Just as the Trojan troops were sure they had the ships within their grasp, they felt a roaring wind and the storm as Poseidon passed through their lines into the Greek camp.

Poseidon, the Earthshaker, found Ajax and told him that the Greeks would hold the rest of the line, but reinforcements were needed. Hector must not be allowed to force the final defenses and come close enough to the ships to burn them.

Helmet to helmet, spear to spear, shield to sloping shield, they stood and waited as Hector and his men leapt for them and were repulsed.

The Greeks broke the charges of the enemy as a huge rock will break the biggest waves in a storm.

Poseidon goaded the Cretan chief, Idomeneus. "What happened to your boasts of driving the Trojans back into their own burning city?"

Idomeneus replied proudly, "We have not broken ranks. Nobody has shown cowardice and run away from this terrible battle. We will not die here to be carrion for Trojan dogs!"

Idomeneus called to his squire to come quickly. They moved to reinforce the left flank. When the Trojans saw Idomeneus coming, fierce as a flame, they attacked him mob-handed.

So it went on beneath the curving sterns of the ships. The killing fields were filled with long, flesh-cutting spears, and the sun dazzled eyes with its reflections off bronze shields and breastplates.

Through all this Achilles sat and sulked.

Idomeneus flung himself into the attack, determined to bring down the night on as many Trojan eyes as possible. Meriones fought hard. Ajax fought like a god. Menelaus caught Peisander the Trojan with his sword, just above the nose. He reeled and fell, and Menelaus stripped him of his armor.

But with so many great fighters wounded, it was hard for the Greeks. Odysseus, Diomedes, and Agamemnon were all hurt. Agamemnon suggested again that they should head for the sea.

Odysseus was furious. "How do we drag our ships into the water with the Trojans at our backs with spears and swords? It's not even practical. We have no choice but to fight."

Poseidon heard this and rejoiced. Disguising himself as an old man, he spoke as if he knew them all well. "My lords, you must not think all the gods are against you. I promise, the day is coming when the Trojans will flee back across the dusty plain to hide behind their city walls."

Poseidon, himself again, roared his battle cry and put fresh courage into all Greek hearts.

Hera had been watching from Olympus and was pleased to see her brother Poseidon busy on the battlefield. She also saw Zeus sitting apart on Mount Ida, plotting how to help the Trojans. She hatched a plan to distract Zeus and to give the other gods a chance to intervene.

Hector and his warriors broke the Greek lines. They carried smoking torches closer to the ships. Hera had little time.

The Trojans raised their flaming brands high and edged closer.

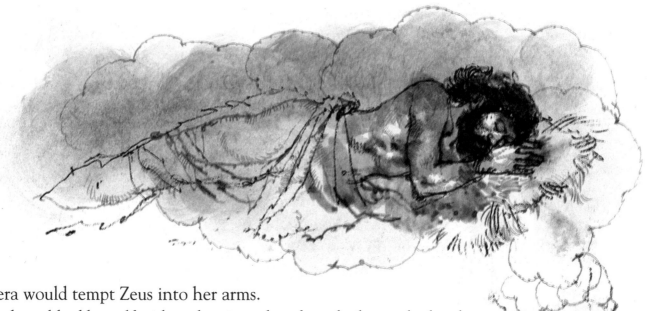

Hera would tempt Zeus into her arms.

First, she rubbed herself with ambrosia and perfumed oils, combed and braided her hair, and put on a glorious robe that Athena had made for her. She added gold and amber jewels, and a headdress of three thousand tiny, golden filigree pieces.

Hera called Aphrodite and asked her for the Girdle of Desire.

"I am going to stop Zeus from interfering," she said.

Aphrodite laughed and gave her the girdle. Hera hurried to find Thoas, god of sleep. Thoas argued he was too frightened to interfere.

"Zeus will cast me into Chaos."

Hera promised, "You can have one of the Graces as a wife."

Reluctantly, Thoas agreed to help.

Hera went to Gargarus, the highest peak of Mount Ida. She knew Zeus saw her coming across the Cretan Sea. She knew he desired her as he had when they first met, and that Zeus was losing interest in the struggling men running around like ants far below him. He had decided that if these men were left alone, victory would go where he wanted. And Hera was looking particularly lovely. . . .

She suggested he might prefer somewhere more secluded.

"We won't be seen, Hera my dear. I will bury us in soft, golden clouds."

They walked down the slopes hand in hand and lay together. Then Thoas crept quietly to them, and the earth sent up fresh grass, lotuses, roses, crocuses, and glorious blood-red poppies.

Zeus slept.

XVII · PATROCLUS GOES TO WAR

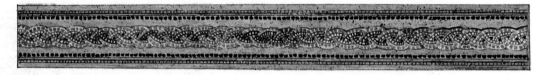

Poseidon watched and took his chance. The Greeks, with his help and the mighty powers of Ajax and Idomeneus, forced the Trojans with their flaming torches away from their ships and back toward the ditch.

When Zeus awoke and saw what had happened, he was furious. He tipped the scales the other way—and now the Trojans were once again inching forward, torches held high, closer and closer to the ships. Hector fought again with Ajax.

Achilles still sulked beside his high-prowed boats while his warriors grumbled. They lived to fight.

Patroclus came to him in tears.

"What's the matter with you, my boy?" Achilles asked his friend. "Don't tell me you're weeping because the Trojans are winning. You know the wrong Agamemnon did to me."

"I'm not weeping for them so much as for you, Lord Achilles. I weep because you are behaving like an evil man, abandoning all Greeks here to eternal darkness. At least let me go into battle with our men."

Achilles shrugged indifferently. Patroclus went on. "Let me wear your armor and take your horses Xanthus and Balius, the wind-runners. The Trojans will think it's you for a moment and give our allies a chance to recover."

Achilles was moved by the young man's courage. "You have my permission. Take my armor and prepare yourself."

Patroclus smiled then and began to strap on the glittering bronze armor, silver-studded and decorated with inlaid gold. He began to look like Achilles, the destroyer of men. Achilles spoke to his warriors.

"My men, my wolf warriors, your time has come. I know you've been chomping at the bit. You've been angry with me. Now you have

70

real work to do. If they set fire to our ships, we are all doomed to die on this beach among the smoldering hulks. Go do the work you know so well."

They lifted their shields in salute and, with Patroclus at their head, moved in close order. Like a woven carpet, they packed together to go into battle. Man to man, shoulder to shoulder, helmet to helmet, they marched into the fight.

Hector watched them coming. He thought he saw Achilles at their head and did not hesitate. He slashed with his sword at Ajax and cut the shaft of his spear. Ajax and his men backed away as the Trojans began to throw their flaming brands into the nearest open ships. In some, tar and rigging quickly ignited and the wood began to burn.

"Patroclus," called Achilles, "save the ships and then drive their warriors to Troy. Come back safe."

And so it began again.

Zeus, looking down, answered part of Achilles' prayer.

Patroclus drove the Trojans from the ships, but as for coming back safely from the battle . . . that was another matter.

When the fresh warriors fell on them, the Trojans saw a fierce man in Achilles' armor, and just as Hector had, they believed they saw Achilles himself. They broke ranks and ran.

After them raced the baying hordes who had come new to the hunt. Harrying, cutting, slicing, charging down their enemies, the wolf-wild men came. Dust rose over them, pierced by the glint and shimmer of bronze on bronze, the screams of dying men, and the unending roar of warriors, as if thunderous surf were roaring over the plain toward the walls of Troy.

Patroclus cut the Trojans off from their city and slaughtered them at will to avenge Greeks already dead. He searched for Hector in the fury of the battle, but Hector had fast horses and kept well away until the gods gave him a sign.

Patroclus hurtled in his chariot behind the wind-flying horses to confront troops led by Sarpedon, a Trojan hero. The two men leapt in full armor from their chariots. They stalked around each other like fighting birds, heads high, spears like claws, screaming death in each other's faces.

Zeus, sitting beside Hera, looked down and was distressed.

"What do you see, my lord?" she asked.

"I see that Fate is unkind. Sarpedon, whom I love, is about to be killed by Patroclus. I could snatch him away and transport him alive to Lycia. Or do I let him suffer his fate? It is hard, Hera, to be all-powerful."

Hera shrugged. "You amaze me. You think of interfering with the fate of a mere mortal? Do it if you want, but be prepared for others to want the same from you. Let Sarpedon die, and then let Death and Sleep take him home to burial and honor."

Zeus sighed and sent bloody rain to fall around the battlefield as Sarpedon cast his spear. It hit the lead horse, which fell and threw the other horses into confusion.

Patroclus threw his spear and hit Sarpedon where the ribcage covers the heart. He fell like a giant oak. Before he died, Sarpedon called to his men to protect his body from the shame of capture.

Patroclus put a sandaled foot on Sarpedon's heaving chest and hauled the heavy spear from the dying man's flesh. The Greeks fought to take Sarpedon's armor and to desecrate his body.

Hector looked across the chaos as his men tried to escape the terrible onslaught.

Patroclus approached the walls of the city, and three times the god Apollo threw him back. Then he warned Patroclus, "Get back. Troy won't be captured by you, nor by Achilles, who is a far better man."

Patroclus fell back a little.

Then the god whispered to Hector, "The time is right. Attack Patroclus. Kill him."

Hector, ignoring other skirmishes, charged through the battle after Patroclus, who wore Achilles' shining armor.

The sun was past its height. The dark shadows of the Trojan walls loomed over the plain. Even as dusk came, great men died and were stripped of armor and of weapons by their enemies.

Patroclus went like a madman into the thickest fighting to kill and kill again. Covered with blood, he speared and gutted man after man, sending them all into an eternity of darkness.

All the while, Hector was moving closer.

Suddenly, Apollo ran past and hit the brave Patroclus between his shoulders. He fell to the ground; his helmet rolled away, smeared with dust and blood. He lost his mighty war spear, and Apollo even unfastened his dented, shimmering breastplate.

Patroclus struggled to his knees, and a Trojan warrior thrust a spear between his shoulder blades. Somehow, his men kept off the attacker, and Patroclus managed to creep away through the lines of his roaring warriors.

Hector, seeing his chance, came screaming through the choking melee. He struck the wounded man in the gut with appalling force. Patroclus fell with a thud to his knees.

Before he died, he looked into Hector's thrusting face and said, "It was not you who killed me. Fate did that. Apollo, who took my breastplate, and hateful destiny did that. But hear me. You have not long to live. You will die soon at the hands of Achilles of the wind! Achilles! Achilles, son of Thetis."

And he fell, face to the sky. So Patroclus died.

XVIII · ACHILLES' GRIEF

Deep, deep under the corals and beyond the white sand, the sea swirled, the light coruscated, refracted, and expanded as the waters broke overhead on the dark rocks. Beyond the land's edge, in translucent shafts of dark green and silver water, Thetis, mother of Achilles, sat surrounded by sea nymphs. Through the depths, she heard a cry of despairing grief echoing around the world.

Achilles sat alone by his black-prowed ships as the son of Nestor ran to him across the hot sand, jumped an anchor rope and then a pile of oars, and stopped before Achilles, gasping for breath. Achilles looked up and saw the news in the boy's eyes.

"Patroclus is dead! They are fighting around his naked body. Hector has your armor. They have sworn to take his head and leave the body at the foot of the Trojan walls for the dogs to dishonor."

Achilles cried out then, and deep under the swirling, wine-dark waters Thetis was already coming to comfort her son. She found Achilles kneeling, clawing up the earth and the ashes from the fire and pouring them over his head in grief at his friend's death.

Thetis tried to raise her son's head.

"My dear son, Zeus has given you some of what you prayed for. The Greeks are no longer penned in close to their ships."

"I have lost my dearest friend, Patroclus, whom I loved as much as I love life. You have lost a son."

"No," she said gently. "Not yet, dear Achilles."

"I'll find Hector, who killed my friend, and kill him. It will be the price he pays."

Thetis shuddered and wept.

"Then I shall lose you—for you are doomed to die after Hector has been killed. That is your fate."

Achilles looked up then and confessed that he had not done his duty by his comrades. "I am their best man, and I have sat by my boat like some crippled watchman."

He spoke to his mother of his grief, and of the smoke of anger that surged through him. "It's like blood pounding in my head, as it did when Agamemnon took Briseis from me."

Achilles sat up and touched his mother's lovely hair.

"I will find Hector. And make all of Troy weep. Do not try to stop me."

"Hector is wearing your armor, stolen from the body of your friend," said Thetis.

Achilles waited.

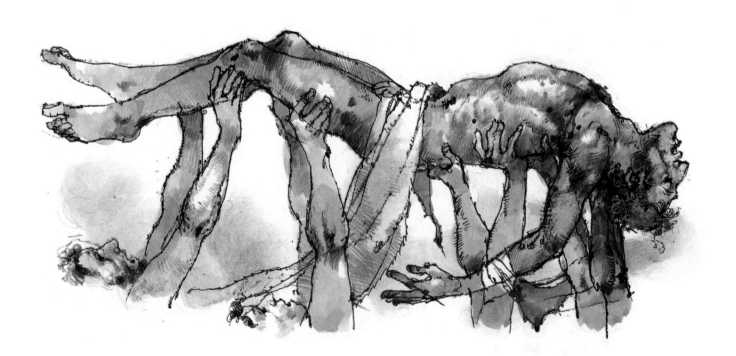

"You shall have such armor as no mortal ever had. I will go to the poppy fields of Cyprus and find the crooked-legged god Hephaestus at his forge. He will remember me and will make what you need. Meanwhile, show yourself to the Trojans. They will be terrified at the mere sight of you. But you must promise not to strike a blow until I come back with all you need."

Out in the stinking battlefield, around Patroclus' naked body, Menelaus, Meriones, and Ajax battled on. In a brief pause, Meriones and Menelaus leaned down to their dead comrade and lifted him shoulder high. They turned then, and carried the bloody body from the battlefield.

Hector harried them like a vulture worrying a piece of meat as they took the body of Patroclus back to his friend, Achilles.

They strode through the roaring noise of battle, protected by Ajax and their soldiers. Men stopped the bloody business of war as the body passed them. A profound silence lay over the plain before the city.

As they strode on to the beach, a huge bird passed overhead.

For a moment, it seemed as if the sun had gone from the world.

XIX · ACHILLES' ARMOR

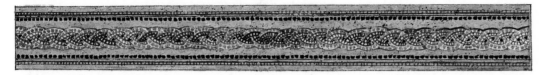

When Hephaestus was born, twisted and monstrous, his mother had wanted to abandon him, but he was rescued by Thetis. Now she found her old friend working at his forge.

"Thetis, Goddess of the Silver Feet, I am honored and you are welcome. You must rest after your long journey."

"I don't have time. Please, stop what you're doing and make a suit of armor for Achilles, my son," she said. "Hurry."

"I can't refuse you." Hephaestus put a grimy hand on her arm. She smiled at him, though her eyes filled with tears.

He turned his sooty face back to the forge and leaned on the bellows. As the fire burned brighter, he chose the metals to make the breastplate, the leg guards, and the plates to cover each shoulder of the powerful hero—fine gold, tin, copper from Cyprus, iron, and silver. He looked at Thetis and smiled, teeth white against the charcoal sweat of his cheeks.

The flames glowed as he turned metal bars in the fierce flames.

On the beach outside Troy, Achilles had Patroclus prepared for the burial rites. "Protect him with herbs and dress him in a white robe. Put his spears and swords at his feet. We will build a vast pyre, lay him with all he owns, and burn him to white bones. They will lie peacefully in his home. But not before I have destroyed Hector, who killed him."

On the battlefield the Trojans, spurred on by the death of Patroclus, pushed back the Greeks. Achilles, remembering that his mother had told him to show himself, went to the top of the wooden palisade.

Alone he stood, a huge man with his long hair flying in the wind. He had neither sword nor spear in his hand. He had no armor on his breast or around his waist. The sun was setting behind him as he looked out over the battlefield and called a challenge to the enemy.

"HECTOR!"

Seeing him silhouetted against the red sun, the Trojans were afraid.

"HECTOR!"

The sun set and the sea blazed with fire.

Hephaestus finished the armor. Thetis marveled at the beauty this ugly giant had created. Into the shield were worked the faces of Earth, Sun, and Moon. Around the rim the constellations ran. The breastplate, shield, and broad-bladed sword were glorious.

Thetis took the armor and brought it to Achilles with aching heart. If Hector died, so would her dearest son.

The Trojans whispered among themselves as they sat around their fires. They had seen Achilles and feared what the next day would bring.

Hector spoke. "Even if he joins the battle, he comes too late. Their men are exhausted. The gods are against them, but with me. Troy will not fall," Hector promised. "I have no fear. None. Nor should you."

He stood there glinting golden in the flickering light of the fires. His armies cheered him as he sent them to their suppers with the promise, "We will attack and destroy them."

Briseis walked from Agamemnon's ships to Achilles. She admired the armor. The flames from the fires made the engraved figures seem alive. It fit him perfectly. Achilles said, "I will make my peace with Agamemnon. I will go to war."

XX · ACHILLES AND HECTOR

Dawn revealed the sleeping figures of the Trojan army spread around the plain. It ate the shadows of the Greek ships standing proud along the beach. Light inched across the cold sand and banished the shadows of the mighty walls. Men stirred, blew life into their small fires, warmed their stiff, cold legs and hands, and looked around them. Each knew in his heart that, if he lived, he would remember this day for ever.

The pale light grew stronger, fragmenting across the constantly trembling ocean. Men began to reach for swords, shields, breastplates.

Achilles greeted the sun, prayed by the bier holding the body of Patroclus, and stepped into the growing light. He called the men together. Odysseus hobbled toward him with Diomedes, using spears as crutches. Agamemnon came and sat a little way apart. They gaped at the armor Achilles wore. The sun glinted, bounced, glittered and shimmered across his bronze and silver breastplate. Achilles spoke.

"My Lord Agamemnon, this killing has gone on too long. Today, I will go back to war."

There was a moment of silence; then the men, their hearts lifted by what they heard, howled their approval, thumping sword hilts on shields like the drums of war. Achilles was back.

Agamemnon rose as the noise died away, and he spoke.

"My judgment was blinded by Zeus, by Fate, and by my own anger. You should know, Achilles, that what was promised you is yours. Briseis, who was brought to me against your will, has already been returned."

The men began to cheer again, but Achilles held up his hand.

"Agamemnon, King of Men, we are wasting time when we could be doing battle. I say we go and take mighty-towered Troy, the lovely Helen, and the spoils that city promises. I will take Hector and leave his body for the carrion crows and dogs."

Once more the soldiers howled their approval.

Odysseus stood then and leaned on the butt of his spear.

"Our men need to eat before they fight, Achilles. They are lesser men than you and need food and drink for strength. And a sacrifice to the gods would be a good idea, Agamemnon, King of Kings."

While they ate and drank some wine, Agamemnon took a black boar down to the sea and sacrificed it with his bronze-bladed sword.

The army gathered. Helmets high and rosy-plumed, great-bladed battle spears on strong ash staves, shields fiery in the morning light, they came marching up from the beach and onto the plain.

In Troy, they heard the marching feet and the thunder of sword on shield. From the city walls King Priam stood watching with Hector's wife, noble Andromache, and Helen, for whom the armies died. They saw the chariots and their prancing horses advancing, the armies marching to the thunder of hooves and war drums.

Closer to the city the Trojan army looked down at their enemy and saw implacable, dark-faced Achilles riding toward them in his chariot. He had the look of a death-bringer about his blazing eyes.

Achilles raised his spear and cried to the roaring horde, "I know I am doomed to die here. But I will not retreat. . . . I will not stop until I have given those Trojans their fill of bloody war. . . . Now, my comrades—CHARGE!"

The Greeks fell on the Trojan army, and Achilles searched in the chaos for Hector.

Zeus, seeing all this, hurriedly gave the gods permission to join whichever side they liked. Then he sat back, took a sip of ambrosia from a golden beaker, and looked down over the roaring armies.

Hera and Athena hurried to the Greek side. Poseidon, the Wavemaker, and Hephaestus followed them, and so did Hermes, the Luck-bringer.

Ares, Artemis, and Aphrodite joined the Trojans.

The two armies leapt at each other's throats. The ground and mountains shuddered. Even in the Underworld, the King of the Dead was terrified by the clash of arms and men.

Achilles turned to his men and urged them on. Then he ran amok, and the earth around him was black with blood, and sticky with it.

Chariot wheels spurted blood from the ground, covering the flanks of horses and the wheels and sides of Achilles' chariot as he dealt death to any who dared to stand against him.

Hector boasted that he was not afraid to confront Achilles, as the Greeks hurled the Trojans back to the walls of their city.

High over the main gates, King Priam watched in horror as the slaughter went on against the very stones of Troy. He saw his beloved son Hector trying to rally the men. Helen, on the same walls, looked for Paris and did not see him.

King Priam ordered that the gates of the city be opened to allow the retreating Trojans sanctuary. Achilles swept them toward their city, then thought he saw Hector running the other way.

He gave chase, allowing the Trojans to crush through the huge gates. Only then, the Trojans safe, did Apollo reveal himself. He had disguised himself as Hector. Furious, Achilles turned and raced back to the city.

King Priam, watching him run, was dazzled by Achilles and his bronze armor. Andromache saw her husband, still outside the walls and in danger from the fast-footed Achilles.

Priam called down to his son not to fight this man alone. "He is a savage, Hector. Come into the city, comfort your wife and your son. Pity me and do not throw away your life. If that man gets inside our city, all of us will be enslaved or dead. It is not fitting that an old man be left for the dogs to defile his nakedness. Come into the city, Hector. . . . Come!"

Priam cried out again. Hector took no notice.

His mother cried out, and then his wife.

Still mighty Hector stayed to confront the figure running toward him, coming closer, closer. He thought, "If I go into the city, I will be called a coward by the very worst of them. I have to stand and fight."

Fleet-footed Achilles was almost upon him. He looked as if he were on fire—the sun struck his bronze armor, and points of light flickered off his spearheads and the sword blade like tongues of flame.

Hector turned then and, as Achilles ran, so *he* ran from the raging Greek, around the walls of the great city. Hector ran, believing that, latecomer to the war as he was, Achilles would be easily worn out. He had forgotten that Achilles, known as Fleet Foot, could outrun horses.

Twice Achilles chased Hector around the city, then once more until Athena came to Achilles and told him it was time to stand and fight.

"Get your breath back, Achilles," she said, then went to Hector to persuade him it was time to confront Fate and fight.

"Achilles," called the panting Hector, "I won't run anymore. I'll fight and kill or be killed. Can we, though, agree among ourselves and our gods? If Zeus allows me to kill you, I promise no outrage will come to your body. All I will do is strip you of your armor, and I will give your corpse to your men untouched. Will you do the same for me?"

Achilles could not believe his ears.

"You must be insane. I'd sooner eat my mother's heart than agree anything with you. I won't rest until your blood floods the gates of Troy. You must pay the price for killing my friends."

Achilles hurled his spear, but held one in reserve.

Hector ducked, and as the spear flew over him, he mocked Achilles.

"Out of practice, of course. You're nothing but hot air and pretty armor. Take this and eat it."

Hector swung his long spear back and thrust it forward powerfully and straight enough to hit Achilles' shield. The spear bent on the bronze boss. Achilles was not hurt.

Hector had no second spear. He drew out his bronze-bladed sword and charged.

Achilles protected himself with his shield and searched the charging man for a place to aim the point of his spear. There was an opening in the armor below Hector's chin. Achilles drove the war spear at this tiny target, and the rushing Hector thrust himself onto it. He dropped like a bull to the bloody ground at Achilles' feet.

Achilles looked down at his writhing enemy, curling and twitching on the spear that now pinned him to the earth.

"You killed my friend Patroclus, so you will pay for that. The dogs and carrion birds will gnaw your guts, while Patroclus burns on his pyre with due reverence to the gods."

Hector, choking on the spear shaft, begged Achilles to be merciful and to let his father, Priam, ransom his body so that his wife and his mother could do honor to him.

Achilles refused. "You'll feed the dogs below your own city walls."

Hector reminded him that he, too, would sometime die, and that the gods would not forget what he had done to Hector, son of Priam.

Achilles laughed in his face.

Hector writhed on the spear and died.

Achilles, to his shame, slit the flesh behind the dead man's ankles, pulled a thong through them, and tied him behind his chariot.

Hector's mother, his father, and his wife saw Achilles drive the chariot three times around the walls of the city, hauling the dead Hector, his head thudding over sand and rock. King Priam looked down from the stone walls and wept. He saw Greek soldiers run to wonder at the size and beauty of mighty Hector. Each of them boldly kicked the naked hero, thrust a sword or a spear into him, and mocked him shamefully.

Andromache wailed a wild ululation of pity, shame, anger, and the horror of knowing her dead husband would not be properly washed and prepared and prayed over.

She unpinned her hair, letting it fall around her face as she knelt on the ground. She lifted handfuls of dirt and poured them over her raven head. She raked her face with her long fingernails, to streak her cheeks in blood, then took up more dirt and scattered it as she cried, "Hector! I will burn your grave clothes we keep in scented chests at home. . . . You will lie naked for the worms to work on and the dogs to eat. . . . Your children have no father and I no protector. . . ."

Again and again, at the gates of the mighty city, she scraped up the black dirt with her bloody nails and poured it over her head.

And the sun fell behind the proud ships, beyond the plain, beyond the mourning city.

XXI · ZEUS INTERFERES

In the morning, the gates of the city remained locked, and down on the beach the proud ships remained propped on their keels. It was as if the world without Hector had changed and even the gods were resting.

The sea was still, but for a tiny ripple at the edge as it softly rose and fell—breathing. Achilles looked out over the pale sea, mourning his friend.

A company of men and mules searched for driftwood and logs. Tall oaks were felled, split, and dragged to the shore where Achilles stood.

Patroclus' corpse was brought in procession, embalmed and sweet-smelling, and placed on the pyre. Around it, offerings were laid. Two-handled jars of honey and oil, four horses, and two of the dead man's dogs were placed beside him. Then Achilles did something terrible. He sent twelve brave Trojan prisoners on the same journey and placed their bodies on the pyre.

The gods sent an eager wind to kindle the fire. The billowing smoke could be seen inside Troy.

Achilles had promised to give the corpse of Hector to the dogs, and would have done so had not Aphrodite protected it with perfumed oils and hidden it in a sea-mist.

Funeral games were held as a pall of smoke lifted into the pale sky and reached as far as Olympus, where Apollo complained to Zeus.

"Achilles is getting up each morning, harnessing his chariot horses, then dragging Hector's body around the barrow they have made for Patroclus. It is shameful."

Hera tried to argue that it did not matter, that Achilles, son of a goddess, could do as he wanted, but the Thundermaker roared at her, "Not if I say he shall not."

Zeus sent for Thetis. "Tell your son, if he refuses to return Hector's body to Priam, his father, he risks my fury. Remind him," Zeus muttered cruelly, "that he doesn't have much longer to live himself."

Thunder rumbled around the mountaintops and sheets of lightning lit the sky as Thetis hurried away to Achilles, who sat at the water's edge, throwing stones into the sea. "Achilles," she called, "it does you no honor to treat the body of noble Hector as you do."

Achilles turned away angrily.

"You will listen to your mother. Zeus is angry. Look over the water and see," and she pointed at the shimmering lightning. "Zeus orders you to accept a ransom from King Priam."

Across the water, thunder rumbled from one side of the sky to the other. Achilles nodded and bowed his head.

"Very well. If that is what I must do, let it be."

He sighed and lifted his head. The lightning stopped, the thunder died away, and a soft wind blew over the sea.

XXII · A BRAVE OLD MAN

In Troy, in King Priam's palace, there was only the constant sibilance of women weeping. Andromache sat in her room, staring at the wall, tears running down her begrimed and bloody face.

Hector's mother sat on the terrace outside the window and refused to eat or drink, or even to speak with her broken husband, King Priam. Hector's children watched and whispered to each other from time to time.

At last, King Priam slept.

Iris came to him in a dream with a message from Zeus. "Priam, know that Zeus wants you to ransom your son from Achilles. Take courage, take suitable gifts, and you will succeed. Go alone."

Priam stirred in his sleep.

"Take one old servant to drive a cart filled with your gifts, and large enough to bring back your brave son's corpse. You will have the protection of Hermes until you reach Achilles' hut. After that you will be alone with him. He will not kill you. Nor will anyone else. Achilles fears Zeus."

Priam awoke and told his family, "I am going down to the Greek ships to ask Achilles to release Hector's body."

The family were terrified he would come to harm, but Priam refused to listen. He gathered up the richest clothes and household goods, the best cooking pots, a jeweled cup from Thrace, as well as pieces of gold plate.

Trojan citizens told him he was a fool to believe Achilles would not kill him. Priam raised his staff and ordered them to leave his palace.

"This is my son. Go! Mind your own business. If I am meant to be killed by Achilles, then I will gladly die beside my son. Just leave me to do as I will." He then turned on his other sons.

"I wish you were all dead and Hector lived. Three brave sons I lost in this war. Mestor, Troilus the charioteer, and now the godlike Hector."

King Priam looked around and saw Paris standing beside Helen.

"Paris, you will fill the cart with treasures. Then I'll leave. I can't bear the sight of you."

As soon as the cart was filled with the ransom, Priam's wife came to him with a golden cup of fine wine, so that he could make a libation to Zeus to ensure his safe return.

"I don't want you to leave me, husband. But as you must, please send a prayer to Zeus, son of Cronos, and ask for an omen to be sent as you ride down to the Greek lines."

Priam poured the libation and made the prayer.

Zeus heard his words.

As the gates of the city opened and Priam and his old servant rode out alone on the mule cart, Zeus sent a hunting eagle soaring high in the darkening sky as a good omen.

The sun was sinking beyond the edge of the world as Priam approached the Greek ships. It was undoubtedly dangerous for the old man and his servant. They stopped to rest the mules and to let them drink. A man came out of the shadows. How could they know it was the god Hermes, come to ease their way?

Priam told him they were looking for Achilles, and Hermes agreed to escort them. They made their way through the lines, invisible to the sentries and the Greek warriors until they came to Achilles' hut.

Old Priam stretched, climbed down from the wagon, and walked toward the hut. Hermes opened the door and stood in the doorway as the hooded figure went in.

Achilles was feasting when Priam strode into the light of the cooking fire. To the astonishment of the others there, the old man immediately knelt in front of Achilles and kissed his hands—the hands that had slaughtered his sons.

"Achilles, think of your own father and what he would have felt if he were in my place. I had the best of sons, and not one worthy of the name is left to me. Please remember the gods and pity Hector's father. I have humiliated myself by kissing the hand that killed my sons. Surely that must be enough."

Remembering his own father, Achilles lifted the crouching figure and wept as Priam wept. Then he spoke quietly to the old man.

"To have dared to come here alone shows who it was who made Hector what he was. Men are wretched things, and the gods make sure we suffer." He smiled gently at the old man. "Remember, sir, that mourning for your son will not bring him back and that you have more life yet. Please sit down and take wine with us."

Priam refused the kind offer, but urged Achilles to accept the ransom he had brought.

Achilles said, "Priam, I have already decided that your son will go back with you."

It happened as Achilles promised. King Priam brought the brave Hector to Troy, and there his body was prepared by his grieving wife, Andromache. She spread sweet oils on the body of her husband. His mother came, and his sisters. Then the body was taken for burning.

It was agreed that no attack would be made while the pyre burned, nor while the white bones were placed inside a golden chest, laid inside a burial pit under a monument of huge stones the Trojans built outside their mighty walls.

But on the twelfth day after the ceremony, Achilles rode his war chariot toward the city, and behind him came his warriors.

The war began again.

EPILOGUE

The siege continued. Achilles struck terror into the enemy and took his men to raid the countryside around the city. The Trojans stayed behind their walls. They had enough food and fresh water; what they lacked was a hero to give them hope.

Priam sent messengers to his half-brother, asking him to send his son, Memnon of Ethiopia. Memnon came.

Tall and brave as a hunting lion, he agreed to fight the Greeks in return for suitable gifts. This warlike man gave courage to the Trojans. They soon roared out of the city, surprising the Greeks and almost reaching the beached ships with their blazing torches.

Achilles was away when Thetis brought him the news: Memnon had challenged any Greek to take him in single combat. And King Nestor's bravest son, a friend of Achilles, had been slaughtered by the Ethiopian. Achilles hurried back to Troy, where Ajax was about to fight Memnon.

Ajax of a thousand battles and Memnon each stood their ground before the gates of Troy. Memnon wore a black-maned helmet, carried a war spear with a sharp-bladed head and a long bronze sword. They stared into each other's eyes and waited for the signal.

Racing across the open plain, Achilles came, armed for combat.

Zeus looked down, holding the scales that balance life and death.

Paris, unseen by any Greek, crouched behind a shield, stared over the dusty plain, and bent his bow. He waited as Achilles stepped down from his chariot and talked to Ajax.

"Memnon is mine, Ajax. He killed my friend, the son of Nestor, my father's friend. I claim the right to do combat with him."

Paris smiled and took a three-barbed arrow from his quiver.

Ajax stepped aside, and Achilles took his place.

Memnon was first to cast his spear. It hit Achilles' shield, bounced off the bronze boss, and lay bent in the dust.

Paris nocked an arrow to his bowstring.

Achilles stepped closer to Memnon, leaned back, his arm fully extended, and threw his spear full force at the Ethiopian's neck.

Apollo nudged the flying spear aside and saved Memnon's life.

Paris fingered his bow, waiting to avenge his brother Hector.

Zeus put a weight in the balance of life and death. It tipped to sentence one of the two fighters to an early journey into the Underworld.

Memnon stepped quickly toward Achilles with his sword ready. Achilles feinted to the left, then to the right and, fast-footed as ever, lunged straight at the advancing warrior. His sword found a space between the breastplate and the silver-studded belt and eased through muscle and gut as the giant warrior ran himself onto Achilles' blade. He dropped like a slaughtered bull.

Achilles turned his back on Troy and raised his hand in triumph.

Seeing his chance, Paris let fly his arrow. It flew as a hawk flies to make its kill—remorseless, eager, unchangeable. It began to dip toward the earth and lose power. Yet still it flew straight and true.

Achilles had been protected from the weapons of men since the time his mother had dipped him in the dark waters of the River Styx. Now, the arrow found the only place her fingers had covered in the whirling waters. It smashed through his heel. It killed him.

So Achilles died at the hands of Paris, who had stolen Helen and caused the war—Paris, whom Hector had called a woman.

With Achilles went all hope for the Greeks. Agamemnon wanted them to leave and go home, to abandon the city of broad streets.

It was Athena who proposed the final cunning solution to the siege.

"All they have to do is get into the city and open the gates to let in the wolf-wild warriors, who want nothing more than to sack and plunder all Troy," she said to Hermes. "Tell Agamemnon to listen when someone comes with a way to open that barred and locked gate."

Agamemnon listened to the cunning Panopeus. He proposed they build a huge wooden horse, fill it with the bravest men, then persuade the Trojans it was an offering to the gods that the Greeks had left when they sailed away.

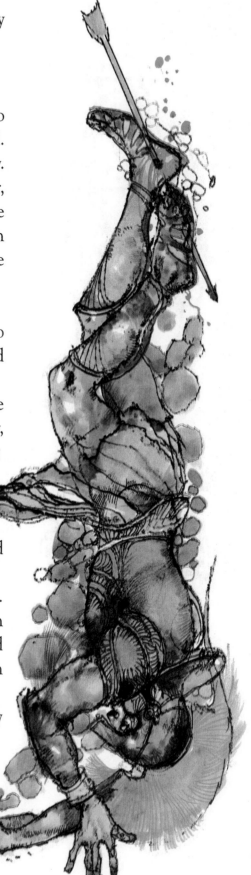

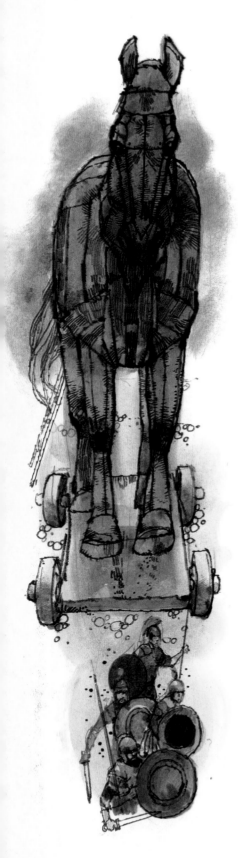

Later, Odysseus said it was his idea. No one could deny it, as all the others there at the time had died, either in Troy or on the journey home. Odysseus was never slow to claim credit. But he was a brave man and agreed to hide inside the wooden horse with twenty-three armed men.

After the horse had been rolled into full view of Troy, Agamemnon burned the Greek camp, ordered the boats to sea, and sailed away.

As dawn broke, the Trojans came to the shore out of curiosity. The ships were gone. The siege was over, and they rejoiced. They found one man still scavenging around the camp. He told them the Greeks had made offerings to the gods and the wooden horse was such an offering. The Greeks had said it was to remain on the battlefield.

The Trojans argued among themselves about the meaning of the horse. Some saw it as a threat. But, eventually, they rolled it into their city, closed the gates for the night as usual, and for the first time in ten years, slept without fear of a Greek attack.

From the belly of the wooden horse the Greek soldiers slipped into the dark streets of the sleeping city. Two men climbed to the battlements, while the rest hurried to the gates in the vast stone walls.

The men on the battlements lit a fire. Agamemnon saw it from far out at sea and ordered the fleet back to the bay below the sleeping city.

The gates were unbarred and opened to admit Agamemnon's troops. Menelaus and Diomedes came with Ajax. All the heroes left alive came like hunting wolves into the city to join Odysseus.

They sacked the city, pillaged riches, butchered men and boys, and enslaved the children and women. Smoke rose in a mighty pall.

Then the fleet, which had been ten years away, sailed back out across the blood-dark sea. Almost all failed to reach home.

Even the wily Odysseus returned only after ten more wild and wandering years. But that is another story.

The city walls are still there, layers of black ash and rubble, the haunt of carrion birds. From Troy came treasures: gold, precious stones, bronze mirrors, gold plates, delicate bracelets, filigree crowns. . . .

Sometimes in the night, the wind howls over the plain. They say it is the souls of those who died and left their blood in the land near Troy.

GLOSSARY OF MAIN CHARACTERS

THE GREEKS AND THEIR ALLIES

Achilles (*ə-kil'-ēz*): son of Peleus and Thetis, commander of the Myrmidons

Agamemnon (*ag'-ə-mem'-nän*): King of Mycenae, brother of Menelaus

Ajax (*ay'-jax*): Achaean commander of the Salamis contingent

Calchas (*kal'-kas*): Achaean prophet, son of Thestor

Cheiron (*kī'-ron*): Most humane of the Centaurs (part man, part beast), healer and teacher, friend of Achilles and Peleus

Diomedes (*dī-ə-mē'-dēz*): King of Argos

Eurypylus (*yū-ri'-pil -əs*): King of Cos

Helen (*hel'-ən*): daughter of Zeus, wife of Menelaus, consort of Paris

Idomeneus (*ī-dō-mē'-nyəˆs*): Achaean commander of Cretans and Pylians

Machaon (*ma-kā'-on*): co-commander of the Thessalians

Menelaus (*me-nə-lā'-us*): husband of Helen, brother of Agamemnon

Nestor (*nes'-tor*): Achaean, King of the Pylians

Odysseus (*ō-di'-sē-əs*): warlord of Ithaca

Panopeus (*pan-op'-ē-əs*): Achaean whose idea it was to build the horse

Patroclus (*pa-trō'-kləs*): Achaean, friend of Achilles

Peleus (*pēl'-yəs*): father of Achilles, King of the Myrmidons

Teucer (*tyū'-ser*): master archer

THE TROJANS AND THEIR ALLIES

Aeneas (*ə-nē'-us*): son of Aphrodite, commander of the Dardanians

Agelaus (*a-jə-lā'-əs*): Trojan herdsman who raised Paris

Andromache (*an-drom'-ə-kē*): wife of Hector

Briseis (*brī-sē'-əs*): daughter of Briseus, captive of Achilles

Chersidamas (*kur-si'-də-məs*): Trojan killed by Odysseus

Chryseis (*krī'-sē-əs*): daughter of Chryses, captive of Agamemnon

Chryses (*krī'-sēz*): priest of Apollo, father of Chryseis

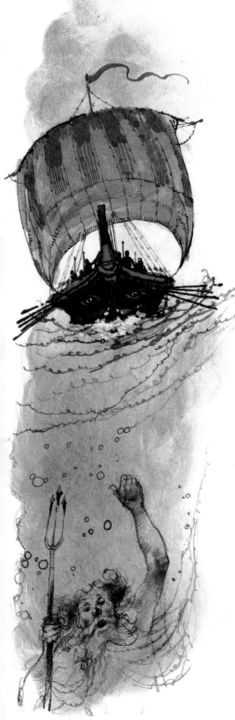

Dolon (*dō'-lon*): Trojan scout

Ennomus (*en'-o-mas*): co-commander of the Mysians

Hector (*hek'-tar*): son of Priam and Hecuba, supreme commander of the Trojans

Iphidamas (*ī-fi'-da-mas*): Thracian killed by Agamemnon, son of Antenor

Memnon (*mem'-non*): King of Ethiopia, nephew of Priam

Paris (*par'-as*): son of Priam and Hecuba

Priam (*prī'-am*): King of Troy, father of Hector and Paris

Rhesus (*rē'-sas*): King of Thrace, Trojan ally

Sarpedon (*sar-pē'-dan*): Trojan ally

THE GODS AND FATES

Aphrodite (*af'-ra-dī-tē*): goddess of love, mother of Aeneas

Apollo (*a-päl'-ō*): god of the sun, son of Zeus and Leto, twin brother of Artemis, principal divine champion of the Trojans

Ares (*ār'-ēz*): god of war

Artemis (*art-a-mas*): goddess of the hunt, daughter of Zeus and Leto, twin sister of Apollo

Athena (*a-thē'-na*): goddess of war and wisdom

Fates (*fāts*): potent, shadowy figures said to control the fate of mortals

Hephaestus (*ha-fēs'-tas*): god of fire

Hera (*hēr'-a*): queen of the gods, wife and sister of Zeus

Hermes (*hur'-mēz*): messenger of the gods

Iris (*ī'-ras*): messenger of the gods

Poseidon (*pa-sīd'n*): god of the sea, younger brother of Zeus

Thetis (*thē-tas*): sea goddess, wife of Peleus, mother of Achilles

Zeus (*zūs*): king of the gods